"I'm not crazy," Derek said, as if reading her mind. "I just…"

He pulled her to his body and she swallowed hard at their closeness. His familiar scent washed over her like a loving caress, her self-control weakening. She might have thought about him all evening, but her thoughts hadn't taken this route. Never had he regarded her with such desire swimming in his eyes. His gaze held hers but quickly lowered to her lips. It was as if he was contemplating his next move. He lowered his mouth closer to hers, but then he pulled back slightly. She wanted to scream, *Kiss me already!* but instead she waited.

His large hands cupped the sides of her face and he mumbled something she couldn't understand. Before she could speak, he captured her lips in a searing kiss. Her thoughts jumbled inside her head. She didn't know what had gotten into him, but whatever it was, she was all in. He kissed her with a hunger that left no doubt they wanted the same thing. At the moment, she didn't care that he wasn't looking for anything long-term. All she knew was that she needed him, desired him right then and there.

Dear Reader,

After *Legal Seduction*, many of you contacted me asking if Iris's sisters would get a story. Well, I'm happy to say—yes!

A Dose of Passion is Macy and Derek's story. You remember Macy, right? Iris's older foster sister, the doctor. Macy longs to fall in love and experience her happily-ever-after and Derek Logan is just the person to help her fulfill her dreams. He just doesn't know it yet.

If you have read my Jenkins Family Series, you might remember Derek. He was first introduced in book one of that series—Craig's older brother. Derek is a single father and his main goal is to raise his son. Life doesn't always go as planned. Not only does he become a millionaire overnight, but he also falls in love when he least expects it.

I hope you enjoy *A Dose of Passion*.

Let me hear from you! (www.sharoncooper.net)

Sharon C. Cooper

A DOSE *of* PASSION

SHARON C. COOPER

HARLEQUIN® KIMANI™ ROMANCE

Recycling programs
for this product may
not exist in your area.

ISBN-13: 978-0-373-86423-2

A Dose of Passion

Copyright © 2015 by Sharon C. Cooper

H HARLEQUIN®

Printed in U.S.A.

™ www.Harlequin.com

Sharon C. Cooper, an award-winning and bestselling author, spent ten years as a sheet metal worker. And while enjoying that unique line of work, she attended college in the evenings and obtained her BA from Concordia University in business management with an emphasis in communication. Sharon is a romance-a-holic—loving anything that involves a happily-ever-after, whether in books, movies or real life. She writes contemporary romance, as well as romantic suspense, and enjoys rainy days, carpet picnics, and peanut butter and jelly sandwiches. When Sharon is not writing or working, she's hanging out with her amazing husband, doing volunteer work or reading a good book (a romance of course). To read more about Sharon and her novels, visit sharoncooper.net.

Books by Sharon C. Cooper

Harlequin Kimani Romance

Legal Seduction
Sin City Temptation
A Dose of Passion

Visit the Author Profile page at
Harlequin.com for more titles.

To the hero in my life (Mr. Cooper)—
thank you for your unconditional love and for making
me feel like the luckiest woman in the world. I love you!

Chapter 1

Macy Carter stood next to the hospital bed and stared down at the man who had been the only thing close to a father that she'd ever had. The man who had been a pillar of strength during some of the most critical times of her life. The man who had beat cancer once, but was now living his last days.

She adjusted the crisp white linen covering him, smoothing out invisible wrinkles and not caring that he hated people fussing over him. Her gaze took in his once-smooth dark skin that now had a yellowish tint. Noah Price was the strongest man she knew, and seeing him like this was like looking at a stranger. So much had changed over the past few months.

A heaviness lodged in her chest and tears pricked the back of her eyes, but she refused to let them fall.

Noah had made her promise that she wouldn't cry over him. As if she could actually keep that type of promise. She was trying. But what was she going to do without him?

She reclaimed her seat next to the bed and rested her head against the back of the chair, closing her eyes. The hospital room was quiet, except for the steady beep of the machines monitoring Noah's vitals, which grated on her nerves more than if the room were full of people talking at the same time. Still, there was no other place she'd rather be than by his side. She would give anything to hear another one of his speeches. *Make the most of your life, baby girl.* She could hear the fatherly advice in her head so clearly. Had it not been for him, she doubted she would have made it through medical school and then her residency. He was everything she needed: supportive, encouraging, and her biggest cheerleader. Looking back on her life in foster care, she wondered what it would have been like to have him in her life from day one. A shoulder to cry on, someone to make her feel secure and someone to teach her about dating and staying away from knuckleheaded boys.

"Macy."

Macy's head jerked up. The single word, barely audible in the stark white hospital room, caught her off guard. For the past two hours, she had sat near Noah's hospital bed and he hadn't spoken a word.

She pushed out of her seat and slowly approached him. "Noah?" She grabbed hold of his limp hand, hoping she hadn't imagined hearing his raspy voice. In the past five days, his health had taken a turn for the worse and the doctors had done all they could do for him. "Noah?"

He opened his eyes and turned to her, gently squeezing her hand. A slight smile tilted the left corner of his lips but disappeared just as quickly.

"Your mother," he rasped. "How did it go?"

A sick feeling flowed through Macy as she thought about the brief conversation she'd had with her biological mother two days earlier. Of all the things Noah could have recalled, she couldn't believe he had remembered her telling him that she had found the woman who had given birth to her.

For the past year, Macy had spent a small fortune paying an investigator to locate Patrice, only to find out the woman wanted nothing to do with her. At two years old, Macy had been placed in foster care after her mother had been arrested for shoplifting and carrying a concealed weapon. Once Patrice was released from jail, she didn't fight to regain custody. Instead, she abandoned Macy, leaving her in foster care.

The slight pressure from Noah's grip on Macy's hand pulled her back to the present.

"Not good. She didn't want to meet, and asked me never to contact her again. She didn't even give me a chance to ask any questions before she hung up on me."

To say Macy was devastated would be an understatement. Granted, her mother had been very young when Macy was born, but not wanting anything to do with her now was unbelievable. What type of mother would disregard her own child?

"I'm sorry, sweetheart," Noah said. His voice was

getting weaker by the day. He had been diagnosed with lymphoma over a decade ago and had been in remission until recently. Despite her and other doctors encouraging him to get treatment, he declined, stating that he wasn't going through chemotherapy and radiation again. The doctors had given him two months, and that was six months ago, but now his health was declining at a rapid pace. "Her...loss." Noah squeezed her hand again. Though his grip was weak, she could feel the love and support that he had always given her over the years.

Macy smiled. Her foster mother, Mama Adel, used to speak those same words whenever Macy got in a funk about Patrice giving her up. Had it not been for Mama Adel and Macy's two foster sisters, Iris and Janna, Macy didn't know where she'd be. The love she felt for those three women often made it feel as if her heart would explode. And then there was Noah. He had been her landlord shortly after she moved to Atlanta and quickly became the father she'd never had.

"Noah, I just can't understand how someone can give up her child and not feel any remorse. She acted as if I was inconveniencing her by even calling."

Macy glanced down at him. His eyes were closed and her gaze moved to the slight rise and fall of his chest. She sighed and pulled away, but he tugged lightly on her hand.

"Better off...without her. Time...to move on." His voice might have been faint, but there was conviction behind his words.

She swallowed the lump in her throat. "Yeah, I know, but it's easier said than done."

But he was right. It was time for her to move on. She was thirty-five, and there were things in her life she had yet to accomplish. One was opening a medical complex and the other, getting married and starting a family. These days, neither goal seemed reachable anytime soon.

Two years ago, Noah had told her that he wanted to help get the medical complex open. Already an owner of several properties in Atlanta, he had been on the lookout for the ideal location and building, or so he had said. Macy had identified several possible commercial properties in the Alpharetta area outside Atlanta, but Noah had always found something wrong with the buildings.

Noah cracked open his eyes. "Where's Derek?" He rubbed his forehead and dropped his hand back onto the bed as if the appendage weighed a ton.

Macy shrugged, not that Noah noticed since he had closed his eyes again. She didn't know where his mini-me had gone, but she was glad he wasn't in the room.

She had officially met Derek six months earlier when Noah had to undergo surgery. Prior to that, she had only heard stories of him. Noah talked about his protégé like a proud father would discuss his son.

Macy still remembered the effect Derek's arrival had on the nurses and hospital staff back then. Tall, muscular, with skin the color of milk chocolate and movie-star good looks, he had a larger-than-life demeanor that sucked the air right out of the room, and Macy had cursed her body for responding.

He was an extremely attractive man, but what held her mind, body and soul captive were his eyes. They were dark and intense, sharp and assessing, making her powerless to look away. Never had a man warranted that type of reaction from her. With this latest visit, he'd been in town for five days, and his presence was wreaking havoc with her senses.

"Derek stepped out." Macy finally answered Noah's question. Noah might have only been Derek Logan's mentor, but almost everything about his protégé reminded her of her surrogate father. Like Noah, Derek wasn't a big talker. There was a quiet spirit about him and she wondered if anything rattled him.

"Noah, do you want me to go and find him?"

He hesitated. "No."

Good. The man was a detriment to her mental peace. When they both were spending time in Noah's hospital room, she kept stealing glances at Derek. He might have been a little standoffish, but he was definitely nice to look at. As far as she was concerned, the less time she spent with him, the better. She had every intention of ignoring the strong pull she felt whenever he was near. She had a feeling he felt it, too. Eyes didn't lie. His appreciative gaze had traveled down the length of her body on more than one occasion.

She shuddered. Yeah, the less time she spent in his presence, the better.

"Craig, I hope you're not teaching my son any bad habits or spoiling him." Derek Logan switched his cell phone to his other ear. He leaned against the sill of the floor-to-ceiling window in the small hospital waiting room, glad to hear his brother's voice.

"Your son is in good hands, bro. I'm teaching him everything I know."

"Yeah, that's what concerns me. I've already had to break him from claiming every girl or woman he meets as his girlfriend." Craig's hearty laugh flowed through the phone line. Sure, he was laughing, but when Jason had asked his teacher to be his date, Derek had been caught totally off guard.

"Well, since I married Toni, Jason and I don't discuss girlfriends."

"Good. He's four years old. As far as I'm concerned, he shouldn't know anything about girlfriends."

"Well, you don't have to worry about that anymore. Now I'm teaching him all about what it's like to have a wife."

Derek shook his head. He knew his brother was joking, but ever since Craig married Toni Jenkins a year ago, all his brother talked about was how wonderful marriage was and how much he loved being a father. Their infant son had mellowed his brother out. As a Cincinnati police detective, he had been wound tighter than a politician on election day before he'd married and had a baby. As far as Derek was concerned, Toni was the best thing that had ever happened to Craig.

"So I assume you're calling to talk to the kid." Craig cut into Derek's thoughts.

"Uh, yeah."

"Well, he's not here. Toni took him and the baby over to her grandparents' house. I'm sure they'll be

back soon. I'll have Jason call you when he comes in."
Derek heard pots banging over the phone line and assumed Craig was cooking. Out of the four of his brothers, Craig was the best chef, though they all could hold
their own in the kitchen. "So how is Noah doing?"

"About the same. His doctor said there was nothing
else they could do for him."

"Ah, man, I'm sorry to hear that. I guess the better
question would be, how are you doing with all of this?"

Derek had always seen Noah as invincible. For fifteen years, Noah had served as his mentor as well as a
father figure, being there for all the big events in Derek's
life. He couldn't imagine his life without the *old man*,
as he lovingly referred to him.

They had met in Cincinnati the summer before
Derek started college. Noah had been a presenter at a
three-day seminar that Derek attended, and they immediately hit it off. When Noah had offered Derek,
who was majoring in architecture, an internship at his
company the following summer, their relationship took
off from there. Derek spent every summer while in college at Price Architectural Firm.

"I'm all right. The whole situation is still a little unbelievable. Before I left his room, he mentioned that he
was tired. I'm not sure if he was just tired…or tired of
fighting." Derek dropped down in a nearby chair, inhaled deeply and released his breath slowly. He'd had
about six hours of sleep in the last forty-eight hours,
and exhaustion consumed his body.

"Well, you know if you need any of us, just say the
word and we're there."

"I know. Thanks, man. I appreciate that. With you taking care of my lil' man, that's all I can ask." When Derek's wife walked out on him and Jason four years ago, he had raised his son by himself, and though at times it was hard, he couldn't imagine not having Jason in his life. He also couldn't imagine not having the support of his family members, who were always willing to step in and help.

"So how are you dealing with, uh, what's her name? Macy?"

"What do you mean?" He glanced at his Movado watch, a gift to himself after he landed a huge contract to redesign an office building a few months earlier.

"I mean, have you gotten to know her better? You do realize that you're not getting any younger, don't you? What better way to get back into the dating scene than with a *doctor*? She could probably teach you things that—"

"Man, I'm not trying to start anything here," Derek said, though he'd been attracted to Macy from the moment he met her. "My main and only focus in Atlanta is Noah. Macy is like a daughter to him, so we're cordial but nothing else. My life is in Cincinnati. You know that."

"You're a freelance architect. You can work anywhere. If she's as hot as you described, maybe you should be trying to get to know her. It's way past time you got back out there and started dating again."

Derek sighed and ran his hand over his head. It seemed as if he was getting the same speech from everyone lately, especially from Craig and their brother

Keith, who was two years older than Derek. He could understand Craig's insistence, but not Keith, who was in the middle of a divorce.

He and Craig talked for a few minutes longer before Derek disconnected. It was time to check on Noah.

The moment he stepped into the room, Macy's pager went off. She glanced at it and blew out a breath. Derek knew she was a pediatrician, but didn't know much else about her, which was okay with him.

If she's as hot as you described, maybe you should be trying to get to know her. Craig's words flitted around in his head. She might have been fine as hell, with blemish-free skin, light brown eyes and a smile that could stop a man in his tracks. But Derek didn't have time for dating, especially dating long-distance. So what if he was curious about whether her long hair was as soft as it looked or that her full lips tempted him beyond belief? He wasn't going to start something he had no intention of finishing.

"When Noah wakes up, can you tell him I'll see him a little later?" Macy asked.

Derek nodded and she surprised him by handing him a business card. They had been keeping vigil over Noah for days and this was the first time she had given him her contact information.

"The hospital knows how to reach me, but can you call me if anything changes?"

Derek accepted the card and glanced at it before returning his attention to her. He had to be careful around her. Those eyes, accented with long eyelashes, could do a brother more harm than good.

"Will do." He slid the card into the front pocket of his pants, his gaze following her as she headed for the door. She had the type of body, curvy without being too skinny or fat, that typically made him take a second glance. She was always casually dressed whenever he saw her, but he could tell that beneath the clothing was a hot body.

He shook his head and chastised himself for allowing his mind to even go there. He didn't need that type of distraction right now.

"You can stop faking sleep, old man," he said when he approached Noah's bed. "She's gone."

"Nobody likes...a smart-ass," Noah said in a voice just above a whisper.

Derek smiled. He hadn't been sure Noah was awake and had spoken the words just for the hell of it.

He took in the older man's appearance. His once-full head of gray, wavy hair was very thin, and his sunken eyes made him almost unrecognizable. Once a large man, Noah barely tilted the scale at a hundred and forty pounds now, and the realization that he was looking weaker by the day unsettled Derek.

"Look out...for her."

Noah's words pulled Derek back to the present. "Excuse me?" He leaned in close.

"You heard...me." Noah's voice suddenly seemed stronger and he met Derek's gaze for the first time in days.

Derek hesitated. There wasn't much he wouldn't do for his mentor, but he wasn't exactly sure what Noah was expecting of him when it came to Macy. He knew they were close, but there was just so much Derek could do for her when he lived thousands of miles away.

"Macy seems pretty independent." He shoved his hands into his front pockets and leaned his hip against the side of the bed. "I'm sure she's going to be fine. Besides, you know I live in Cincinnati. Between my architecture business and Jason, I don't have much time for anything else." Derek shrugged. "I honestly don't think you have to worry about Macy. She's sharp. She'll be all right."

"What about you?"

"What about me?"

"It's time…start living." Noah's wheezy cough sounded as if it was painful, making his whole body shake. "That ex-wife did a number…on you," he rasped. "But it's time…to move on."

Derek groaned and rubbed the back of his neck and strolled over to the single window that was on the other side of the room. Staring out into the night, the last thing he wanted to talk about was his ex-wife. The day she walked out on him and his son was the day he'd vowed to stay clear of emotional entanglements with women.

"Son…I'm tired," Noah said. Derek glanced over his shoulder. Noah looked as if he had aged in only a few minutes. "I need to know…the two of you will be okay when I'm gone."

Derek pushed away from the window and went to stand next to the bed. Yes, he knew Noah was dying. Yet he still couldn't accept the idea of not having him around.

"Promise me…you'll look after Macy. And that you…will start living again." When Derek hesitated, Noah continued, "Promise…me." His voice was almost haunting. Foreboding crept up Derek's spine. "Promise me."

Derek swallowed hard. "Yeah. Yeah, I promise."

Chapter 2

Three days after Noah's memorial service, Derek sat in his mentor's lawyer's office in shock. "He left me Price Architecture?" he said to himself.

No matter how many times Derek said the words out loud, he still couldn't believe it. He rested his head against the high-back leather conference-room chair, trying to process all that Drew Ashton, Noah's attorney, had told him. Noah and his wife had never had children and more than once, Noah had told him that he was like the son he'd never had. Derek now had a good idea just how Noah had felt about him.

Drew had gone through the specifics of the will as it related to Derek. Not only had Noah left him enough cash to live comfortably for years, but he had also bequeathed him a house in one of Atlanta's suburbs. It was the knowledge that Noah had entrusted him with his multimillion-dollar company, his baby, that had Derek's mind reeling, though. Never would he have expected to inherit the company. Sure, he had worked alongside Noah during the summers while in college and even occasionally after graduating, but Derek never expected he would one day be the CEO of the organization.

"Sorry about that." Drew walked back into the luxury conference room and closed the door. The space looked as if the law office had spared no expense in its decor. The wall-to-wall bookshelves against deep taupe walls with dark wood trim gave the room a cozy feel, like a home library, fireplace and all.

Drew reclaimed his seat next to Derek at the round table. "I know this is a lot to take in, but I'm here to answer any questions you might have." He opened the folder that he had brought back into the room with him. "You knew Noah well enough to know that the will comes with a number of stipulations."

"I'm sure it does," Derek said dryly, feeling a little overwhelmed with all that had happened since losing Noah. Overseeing the memorial service was one of the hardest things he'd ever had to do. There were moments in the days since then when he still couldn't believe he was gone. Noah had always seemed bigger than life and Derek had no idea how his life would play out without having his friend and confidant in it.

Derek's gaze dropped to the photo in his hands of the home that Noah had left him. Actually, it was more like a mini mansion. The two-story, five-bedroom, four-and-a-half-bathroom, colonial-style brick house with tall, mature trees and a manicured yard was breathtaking, even on paper.

"As I mentioned, within the next three weeks, you would be required to relocate to Atlanta and live in that house for a minimum of one year. And as for the company, you must agree to take the reins of CEO and maintain ownership of the firm for no less than a year."

"I would never sell Price," Derek said, not meaning to voice his thought aloud. He was honored that Noah trusted him enough to oversee the company. For years, he had tried to get Derek to move to Atlanta and be his right-hand man. Derek hated that it took Noah's death to get him to play a role in the firm.

"Glad to hear that." Drew broke into his thoughts. "I know I don't have to tell you that Noah poured his heart and soul into the company. His staff is more like family, and I think you will find them quite helpful as you get settled in your new role. As a matter of fact, based on what I know of you through Noah, you're the perfect person to take the firm to the next level."

"Thank you." Derek met Drew's gray-eyed gaze before diverting his eyes back to the papers in front of him. He had heard of people becoming millionaires overnight, but never had he imagined it could happen to him. Not only had Noah provided for his future, he had also set up a trust fund for Jason.

Derek shook his head, trying to wrap his mind around everything Drew had shared with him for the past forty-five minutes.

"Attorney Ashton, you mentioned I would have to

move into the home and join the team at Price within three weeks. I'm not sure if I can pick up and move my household in that short amount of time."

"First, please call me Drew. Second, Derek, you are now a very wealthy man, assuming you adhere to all of the stipulations in the will. Noah has left you additional funds to assist you with any and all relocation costs. You'll soon find out money solves a lot of problems and comes in handy when you have to do something quick."

Drew slid a check across the table and Derek's gaze immediately zoned in on all of the zeros behind the five. His mouth dropped open. He fingered the check but didn't pick it up.

"This is just for relocating?"

Drew chuckled. "Actually, that check is yours free and clear, whether you agree to the stipulations in the will or not. Noah wanted you to have something whether or not you decided to relocate and build a life here in Atlanta. So if you decide not to move here and accept the CEO position, you won't walk away empty-handed. Oh, and the trust fund for Jason is not contingent on anything. Noah often referred to him as his grandson."

Derek nodded.

"I know this is a lot to take in, but there's more." Drew closed the folder and, as if on cue, the conference room door opened and his assistant stepped in.

"Drew, Macy is here. Should I show her in?"

"Yes, please do."

Derek cocked his head and looked at the attorney, but before he could pose a question, Macy was standing in the doorway.

Her gaze met his, and it was clear she was just as surprised to see him as he was to see her. She recovered quickly and walked farther into the room and shook Drew's extended hand.

Derek stood and he couldn't stop his gaze from roaming over her sexy body. He hadn't seen her since Noah's memorial service.

Despite a hint of fatigue around her eyes, she was as beautiful as ever. Gone was the ponytail she usually sported, as well as the simple shirt and slacks she preferred for work. Instead, she wore a low-cut red blouse that highlighted her breasts and flat stomach. The short black skirt she wore stopped just above her knees and fit her curves perfectly without looking indecent. In all of the times he had seen her, he'd never realized she owned a pair of shapely, traffic-stopping legs that seemed to go on forever. She had worn a pantsuit to the memorial service, but a woman with legs like hers should show them off every chance she got.

"Derek?"

His gaze shot up when he realized Drew had called his name more than once and gestured for him to reclaim his seat at the round conference table.

Instead of greeting Macy with words, they nodded at each other.

"Macy, please have a seat here." Drew pulled out the chair on the other side of his. "I wanted you both to be here so I could discuss the rest of Noah's will."

Macy restrained from fanning herself at the sight of Derek in a suit. Had she known he would be there, she would have mentally prepared herself. His presence still affected her down to the core of her being. Granted, she hadn't been with someone in months, but how could she be attracted to a man of few words who was also aloof and seemed to want to be anywhere she wasn't?

If only she could forget how good it had felt to be in his strong arms, hugged up against his hard body. She would never forget that day, for more reasons than one. It was a week ago. Derek had called her at work, informing her that she needed to get to the hospital. Noah had passed away before she arrived. Though she knew the day was coming, she hadn't wanted to believe her father was gone. No amount of preparation had prepared her for the loss she felt deep down in her soul. And to be comforted by Derek had wreaked havoc on her emotional state. His long, muscular arms wrapped firmly around her and the woodsy scent of his cologne had her wanting to bury her nose in the crook of his neck for a deeper sniff. The man who she'd thought was unfeeling and distant comforted her with soothing words while he held her close until she was able to pull herself together.

She glanced at him across the table and their gazes collided. It was as if someone had wrapped their hands around her throat and squeezed. She could barely breathe staring into his dark, intense eyes. Diverting her gaze, she returned her attention to Drew, who was speaking and sifting through a file folder on the table in front of him.

"Macy, here's a letter Noah left for you. I'll let you read it now before we proceed."

She hesitated before accepting the white envelope

and fought the urge to hold it against her chest, over
her heart. She had always thought of herself as a strong
person, but the past week and a half had proven she
wasn't as strong as she thought.

She took a deep breath and released it, bracing herself for Noah's last words to her. The last thing she
wanted to do was fall apart in front of Drew and Derek.

She smiled at the sight of Noah's scribble.

My dearest Macy,
If you're reading this letter, it means I have gone
on to a better place…hopefully. I hope you don't
think I forgot about our agreement regarding the
medical complex. I didn't. Drew will give you the
details regarding the building and the renovations.

Baby girl, I hope you know how proud I am of
the woman you've become. You were like a little
girl to me when you first moved to Atlanta for
college, and I watched you grow into an amazing woman. You're the daughter I never had. It's
no wonder people gravitate to you. The love and
compassion you show everyone you meet, as well
as your work ethic, make me proud.

But I worry about you, the way you always put
others first, stretching yourself thin, and you're
the first person people seek out when they have
a problem. Promise me you'll start taking care
of yourself. I know we always got together for
dinner on Thursday nights, but maybe you can
keep that going, just with someone else. Perhaps
with a man your own age?

Macy chuckled at the last sentence and blinked rapidly, fighting off the tears that were threatening to fall.

I want you to have the type of love and passion I shared with Lorraine while she was alive. There's nothing like finding your soul mate and building a life together. It's time for you to settle down and have the family you always wanted. I just hate I won't be there to walk you down the aisle the way we used to talk about or hold your firstborn.

I love you, baby girl. I'll be with you always.
Noah

Macy closed her eyes and held the letter to her chest, unable to hold her tears at bay. She would never hear his deep voice call her "baby girl" again and she felt the loss the same way she had when Derek had first informed her that Noah was gone. She felt so blessed to have had him in her life and he would forever hold a special spot in her heart.

Macy slowly opened her eyes when she felt a hand on her arm.

"Are you okay?" Drew asked. He handed her a box of tissues. "We can give you a moment if you need it."

Derek stared at her openly and didn't speak, but she didn't miss the concern in his eyes. Maybe he wasn't as distant as she had first thought.

"Sorry. I'm all right," she said to Drew and dabbed at her eyes and cheeks. She breathed in deeply and slowly released her breath. Something she did often, especially right before she had to deliver bad news to the parents of her patients. "Thank you for giving me this."

"My pleasure." He squeezed her arm and returned his attention to the papers in front of him. "I'm sure you both have other things to do today, so why don't I explain another part of Noah's will." He handed Derek a large manila envelope and then gave another one that wasn't as thick to Macy. They both opened them and perused the contents.

Macy's heart thumped faster against her chest as she sifted through documents that included a deed and title to a new commercial building that would one day serve as a medical complex. Her gaze fell to the set of keys in her hand. Noah had done it again. He had helped get another one of her dreams started. All she could do was stare at everything, finding it hard to believe what it all meant. He had already left her an obscene amount of money, but to give her a building, too, was unbelievable.

"Wow." The one word slipped through her lips and didn't begin to express the elation flowing through her body. He had told her he was going to help her with the medical complex, but to see his promise come to fruition was beyond exciting.

She glanced at Derek as he went through the contents of his envelope. He also had a set of keys that she wondered about, as well as some drawings and what looked to be a blueprint.

Derek shrugged. "Exactly what am I looking at here?" he asked but didn't look up from the documents.

"That's most of what you will need to get started

working on the medical complex that Noah promised Macy."

"What?" Macy and Derek said in unison, staring at Drew.

"What do you mean, he'll be working on my medical complex?"

Macy sat dumbfounded as Drew explained how Derek would be in charge of overseeing the project from the beginning to the end, including the design, renovations, furnishings and everything else needed to get the doors open.

What had Noah been thinking? Sure, he had told her Derek was one of the most talented and sought-after architects in the country, but did he have to get him involved with her project? Why was he forcing her to work so closely with Derek? Surely he had sensed the tension between the two of them during their visits. How was she going to keep her wits about her if she had to see Derek and be subjected to the hypnotic scent of his cologne whenever they had to meet to discuss the specifics of her ideas?

By the scowl on Derek's face, he wasn't any happier about the news.

God help me. She was going to need to do a lot of praying and probably take some cold showers over the next few months just to get through this new adventure.

Chapter 3

Derek drove into the cul-de-sac and to his new place. The brick colonial, with four oversize pillars and beige trim, was one of the largest homes in the neighborhood, and it was his. He still couldn't believe all that Noah had left him. Derek also couldn't believe he'd packed up both himself and his son and relocated to Atlanta, all within a two-and-a-half-week period. As a single father, raising a child alone was hard enough. Take away his built-in babysitters, and it was like sailing upstream without a paddle.

Now that he had made the big move, the challenges it would bring, raising Jason and getting acclimated to a new city, were at the forefront of his mind. Not only that, but he had started his freelance architecture business a few years earlier and it had recently taken off.

Leaving Cincinnati to oversee Price Architecture was a once-in-a-lifetime opportunity, but he hated that he had to subcontract out some of his own projects before coming to Atlanta.

Derek pulled into the extra-wide semicircular driveway and slowed before he reached the three-car garage. Noah had given the mansion that he'd lived in before passing away to his favorite charity. Derek couldn't understand why he would purchase this home only to risk leaving it empty, considering he couldn't have been sure Derek would agree to the relocation. Noah didn't do anything without a reason, but this part of his will had Derek stumped.

His gaze fell back on the structure of his mini mansion. He couldn't keep the smile from spreading across his lips. Noah definitely knew what Derek liked when it came to houses. Tudors were his favorite, but this colonial-like home was a little unique, with its wide Palladian window above the double burgundy front doors.

He drove farther up the driveway, stopping in front of one of the garage doors before cutting the engine. Part of him was excited about all of the changes to his life, but there was a twinge of anxiousness that spun inside his gut.

"Daddy, why did we stop?"

Derek turned to the backseat where his four-year-old son sat in his booster seat, playing a video game. Jason had been so quiet, Derek had momentarily forgotten he was there.

"This is our new home, son. Ready to check it out?" Derek stepped out and walked around the car to open

Jason's door, but his son didn't budge. Neither of them was overly thrilled about leaving their home and family in Cincinnati, but together they were going to embrace this new chapter in their life. "Let's go, kid."

"Is Uncle Keith here? He said he was coming to my new house," Jason asked as he slowly climbed out of the Mercedes ML63 SUV. Derek's new assistant at Price had surprised him with the vehicle when they departed the plane. He now understood why she had asked him a series of questions the day he met with her. One question had been about his ideal car. Who knew the car of his dreams would be waiting for him? Supposedly, it was part of his benefits package.

"Daddy, is he coming?" Jason pulled Derek back to the present.

Just then, Keith Logan pulled up in a rented SUV that he was using until his car, which he'd had shipped to Atlanta, arrived. Keith parked next to Derek and climbed out of his vehicle.

"Hey, Uncle Keith!" Jason ran to his uncle, who lifted him up in the air. "What took you so long?"

Derek chuckled at his son's enthusiasm. It was as if he hadn't just seen Keith at the airport. They had arrived to Atlanta in style, flying on the company's private jet, a first for all of them, one that Jason would be talking about for weeks.

So far, the relocation was going great. Since his brother was in the midst of a divorce and ready for a new start, Derek had invited him to Atlanta. Keith jumped at the opportunity. It was a win-win for both of them. Derek would get some help with Jason, and

Keith had a potential job opportunity with Price Architecture.

"Looks like a nice neighborhood," Keith said. They stood on the front stoop with suitcases, waiting for Derek to open the door. "A little bougie. So you ought to fit in perfectly."

"Ha, ha, ha. Whatever." Derek pushed the front door open and deactivated the alarm system using the keypad just inside the wide foyer. His brothers had always called him "bougie," claiming he was stuck up despite growing up in one of the roughest neighborhoods in Columbus.

Keith released a long whistle as the three of them stood in the foyer of their new home. Derek had to admit—it was a beauty. The semicircular staircase with ornamental wrought-iron railings and a chandelier made of the same material gave the space a rich, unique feel. A large area rug with a design and colors that pulled from the taupe walls and iron accents partially covered the dark hardwood floors. Whoever Noah had used to renovate the home had nailed his personal style.

"Dang, man, you said this place was big. Heck, it's like three times the size of my house in Cincinnati. What's the square footage?"

"Daddy, where is my room?" Jason started roaming around the empty lower level while Derek and Keith remained where they were.

"Upstairs, lil' man. It's the second room on the left." Jason ran up the stairs and Derek wondered if he understood which room was his. "Oh, and to answer your

A Dose of Passion

question," Derek said to Keith, "we're working with over 3,500 square feet." He picked up the luggage he had left near the front door. "Four bedrooms are upstairs and there are two you can choose from. I'm thinking I'll use the one down here as a guest room."

"I assumed I'd be getting the master bedroom," Keith said with a straight face as they clumped up the carpeted stairs. Out of Derek's four brothers, Keith was the laid-back one that kept the rest of them laughing and on their toes.

"And why would you assume that?" When they reached the top landing, they found Jason in the master bedroom. "Guess you're out of luck, Keith. Looks like someone beat us to it."

"Daddy, my room is big!" Jason said, trying to climb up on the king-size bed Derek had ordered weeks earlier and had delivered. With his assistant Louise's help, he had ordered furniture for his and Jason's bedrooms, as well as for the family room. He had everything delivered a couple of days earlier. Now they were just waiting for the movers to bring some of his furniture from his and Keith's old houses, as well as a ton of boxes. Normally, Derek wouldn't be looking forward to unpacking, but the movers had not only packed up everything for him, but they would also unload everything as well.

"Wrong room, kid." Derek set his luggage near the closet. "Come on. I'll show you where you'll be sleeping."

"Yay! I have two beds," Jason said as he ran into the bedroom and climbed the steps to the top bunk. Since his son was into spaceships, Derek already had some ideas on how they would transform the area. "Look at my room, Uncle Keith."

"Yeah, man. It's big. A lot more space for all of your junk, I mean, your toys." Keith laughed. He left them in Jason's room to go in search of his own bedroom.

Derek stood at the single window looking out onto the front yard and street. He was slowly starting to warm up to the new life he was getting ready to dive into.

Change often comes with gifts, Noah had once said when he first found out about Derek's ex-wife leaving him. At the time, the only gift Derek could see in the situation was Jason. Now that his life had recently been flipped upside down, albeit in a good way, Derek wondered if Noah had started making these plans even back then.

Hours later, Derek strolled outside and sat on one of the steps to his deck. Leaning back, his elbows propped up on the step behind him, he watched his son run around the yard, trying to get his kite to fly. To be young and carefree again. The boy had an endless amount of energy.

Derek closed his eyes and let the beaming sun warm his skin. Long morning. He could honestly say he was exhausted. The past few weeks had been unbelievably busy, and sleep every night hadn't come easy. He couldn't get his mind to slow down. He had so much to do, including finding a preschool program for his four-year-old son in less than a month. And then there was Macy.

Macy. The beautiful, sexy goddess with the long legs and bedroom eyes was sure to be the new bane of his existence. The little sleep he had gotten over the past few weeks included erotic dreams of her either in skimpy attire or nothing at all. He groaned just thinking about her full breasts and curvaceous body. Working on the medical complex with her was sure to prove to be the greatest challenge of the move. He hadn't even started yet and already thoughts of her made a certain part of his anatomy jump to attention. Sitting next to her at the memorial service and then across from her in Drew's office weeks ago left his body reeling.

"Lunch is here," Keith yelled from somewhere behind Derek. "Get it while it's hot."

The three of them ate while Jason kept a steady flow of conversation going, giving Derek and Keith a chance to interject periodically. When it seemed Jason was all talked out, Derek knew his son would be asleep soon.

"I really appreciate you letting me stay here a while. I have a feeling this move is going to be good for all of us." Keith stood and tossed his paper plate in the trash before pulling a beer out of the refrigerator. "Not only do you get someone to help with Jason, but you also get to live like the rich and famous." He emphasized by lifting his arm and waving it around at the large space and twenty-foot ceilings. "And I'll get a fresh new start."

What started as an amicable divorce process between Keith and his wife had turned ugly a few weeks earlier when Keith's father-in-law laid Keith off from work, saying they were taking the company in a different direction. At first, the news couldn't have come at a worse time, but then, with the opportunity to start over in Atlanta, Keith had figured something good could come out of a bad situation.

He had an interview with the finance department at Price Architecture in three days. Though Derek told him he'd have to get the job on his own, he had no doubt that his brother would wow them. The guy was a whiz with numbers and had played an instrumental role in taking his father-in-law's company to the next level.

"I think the lil' man has finally worn himself out." Keith nodded toward Jason, who was asleep in his chair. Derek caught him just in time, before he fell out of his seat.

"I was wondering when he'd clunk out." Derek lifted him. "He's been going nonstop since six o'clock this morning, with only a short nap on the plane."

Derek carried him upstairs. Sitting on the edge of the bed, he ran his hand over his son's soft curly head and stared down at his sleeping form. Jason was the most important person in Derek's world. Sometimes, when he thought about the responsibility of raising a child on his own, it made him nervous. Other times, he wouldn't have it any other way.

He placed a kiss on the top of his son's head and bounded back down the stairs.

"It looks like the movers are finally here," Keith said from the living room window. "But they are a little distracted by the cutie-pie in the tiny shorts next door who's cutting her grass."

Derek stood next to his brother at the window and

pulled down one of the slats of the blinds, stretching his neck to see the person. It wasn't the short-shorts his brother alluded to that he was interested in, though. He hadn't met any of his neighbors yet and hoped there were children nearby that were Jason's age.

"Instead of staring out the window, maybe you can roll up your sleeves and help guide the movers."

"I'd rather go next door and introduce myself to the cute neighbor. Apparently, she doesn't—"

Derek released the slat and started to walk away, but quickly turned back when at the last second he caught sight of the woman behind the lawn mower.

"What the…"

Ignoring the rest of Keith's comment, Derek bolted for the front door. He cleared his four concrete steps with no effort and stomped across his yard and the neighbor's double-wide driveway, not stopping until he was in front of the lawn mower.

"Hey!" Macy yanked out her earbuds and snatched off her sunglasses. "What are you…?" Her voice trailed off and surprise registered on her beautiful, sun-kissed face. "What…what are you doing here?" she yelled over the rumble of the mower before shutting it off. "How did you know where I lived?"

"Like you don't know." The words flew out of Derek's mouth impatiently. He folded his arms across his chest, anger darting through his body. He didn't like games, and apparently she and Noah had a game of their own going on. First, the medical complex project, and now this. "Why didn't you tell me the house Noah left me was next door to yours?"

Her mouth dropped open and she leaned away from him as if he had struck her. "I didn't know Noah left you a house, and I sure as heck didn't know it was that one!" She jabbed her glove-covered finger toward his home. "And how dare you step to me like some crazy madman?" she seethed, her eyes boring into him like a laser beam. "I don't know what your problem is or what you have against me, but I'm sick of it!"

She snatched her gloves off and stepped around her mower, standing only inches from him. He could feel her anger seeping through her pores, right along with the perspiration coating her skin. "You have been a big, brooding…lug," she yelled, frustrated, her hands on her hips. "From the day I met you, you treated me like a piece of gum you've had stuck on the bottom of your shoe. What have I ever done to you?"

Derek studied her, trying to decide if she really didn't know what Noah had been up to. By the way she was shooting daggers with her eyes, it was safe to say she hadn't been a part of Noah's little game.

Instead of answering her question, his gaze traveled the length of her, from her messy ponytail propped on the top of her head to her thin tank top displaying her more-than-a-handful breasts. He stopped at the tiny shorts. When he should've been trying to come up with an answer to her question that wouldn't make him sound like a total jerk, he instead had an overwhelming desire to pull her into his arms and taste her pouty lips.

Damn, he had it bad. The woman's gaze cut into him and all he could think about was having her body rubbed up against his, sweat and all.

"Oh, so now you have nothing to say?" She slapped her gloves against her thigh, seeming to be madder than before. "You are unbelievable. You come over here making this big fuss about something I have no knowledge of and now you're standing there ogling me." She turned and went back to her lawn mower. "Well, I guess that's better than the permanent scowl you wear."

Derek sighed and rubbed his hand over his head and let it slide down the back of his sweaty neck. He didn't know if he would ever get used to the ninety-degree temperature. It was only July. He didn't want to think about how hot it would be in August.

"I don't scowl," he finally said. His words sounded wimpy even to his own ears.

The sharp edge to her humorless laughter made him want to snatch back his words. "You've got to be kidding me." She used her forearm to dab at the sweat on her forehead. "I can understand you being concerned about Noah, but that constant frown you wear on your face whenever I'm around is a good sign that you have a problem with me."

"I don't have a problem with you!" He shoved his hands into the pockets of his cargo shorts and stared down at his shoes, trying to come up with something intelligent to say. What the hell was wrong with him? He was acting as if he were still in high school. She was right about one thing, though. He did have a problem with her. She was too damn *fine* for her own good and he was seriously attracted to her. And he hated it. Now what to do about it was the question.

* * *

The last thing Macy needed was to live next door to the man she couldn't stop thinking about. She didn't want to believe Noah was playing matchmaker from the grave, but what else could she think? First he created a situation in which she would have to work with Derek over the next few months, and now this. How was she supposed to have peace of mind when she knew the tall, dark, brooding man with the sexy, intense gaze was sleeping next door to her? He had already caused her some sexually frustrated, sleepless nights. Now she would probably have to move if she ever wanted to get any rest.

She slipped her gloves and her dark shades back on. She so wanted to be angry at Derek, but how could she be when he towered over her like some sex god? Tall, lean and gorgeous. He looked good enough to make her want to drop her panties, no questions asked. Damn her body for betraying her. His blue fitted T-shirt stretched across his solid chest, hugged his thick biceps and lay flat against his abs. The cargo shorts he wore hung low on his hips, and his thick legs were muscular, like those of a football player. Her gaze finally edged back up his body and landed on his intense eyes. Damn him and his sexy eyes.

"Why are you still here?" she snapped. "I have work to do." Mama Adel would have a fit if she heard her being this mean to anyone. She would always tell her foster daughters there was no excuse to stoop to someone else's level if they were acting a fool.

He looked as if he was trying to determine whether

or not she was telling the truth, but said nothing. His shoulders dropped and he rubbed his forehead.

"I'm sorry," he said gruffly. "I was surprised to see you out here."

"Probably no more surprised than I am to see you standing on my grass, blocking me from finishing my yard." She slipped off her work gloves again and shoved them into the back pocket of her shorts. It seemed as if he was in no hurry to leave her alone.

Swiping her arm across her forehead for what seemed like the hundredth time, she wiped away the perspiration beading at her hairline. *Noah, what are you up to?* Derek moving in next door wasn't a coincidence.

"Are you saying you didn't know that Noah purchased that house and insisted I move into it?"

"I didn't even know the house was for sale. My neighbor, a sweet older woman who was *always* a pleasure to have living next door, told me she had sold the house about a month ago." Macy didn't try to hide the bite in her words. She wanted him to know she wasn't any happier than he was about this new development. "She said someone had made her an offer she couldn't refuse. And despite what you might think, Noah didn't always check with me whenever he decided to do something crazy."

"So you didn't know he was leaving me that house in his will and insisting I move into it?"

Macy's hands flew to her hips. "What part of 'I didn't know' don't you understand? You come over here yelling like you've lost your mind because you think I'm playing some game? Well, I'm not. I don't play those types of games."

"Daddy!" Macy heard the high-pitched voice before she saw the cutest little boy running across the yard toward Derek, not stopping until his arms were wrapped around his leg. "Hi. What's your name?" the little guy asked, hiding slightly behind his father.

A smile tugged at Macy's lips. There was no way this cutie-pie could be related to the big lug. She bent down to his level. "My name is Macy. What's yours?"

"Jason." He finally released Derek and approached Macy. "I'm four. How old are you?"

"Jason." Derek's warning tone caused Jason to glance up at him. "What did I tell you about asking grown-ups their age?"

Jason lowered his eyes and bit on the tip of his finger. "You said it's not appoiate," he said, butchering the word. Macy was impressed he had even gotten that close to saying it correctly.

"Well, it's nice to meet you, Jason." Macy stretched out her hand for a handshake. Jason glanced at his father before accepting her hand and grinned, showing off two missing front teeth and making Macy fall in love with him instantly.

"You want to be my girlfriend?"

"Jason!"

Macy burst out laughing and tipped backward on her haunches, catching herself with a hand behind her before tipping all the way back. She stood to her full height and dusted her hands on her shorts. She didn't know what was funnier, the fact Jason knew anything about girlfriends or the horror on Derek's face.

"What did I tell you?" Derek lifted his son effortlessly, holding him out in front of him. "You are too young for a girlfriend and you are *not* to ask another grown woman to date you. Do you understand me?" Jason nodded slowly and Derek threw him over his shoulder, clearly frustrated but eliciting a giggle from his son. "I'm sorry," Derek said to Macy. "Apparently I need to break some of the bad habits he's learned from one of his uncles."

Macy waved him off. "No harm done. He's absolutely adorable." Thanks to Jason, some of the tension between them seemed to have dissipated.

They stood there in awkward silence. Like her, Derek was probably wondering what was on Noah's mind when he'd purchased the house for Derek to move into. They continued to stand there, each in their own thoughts, until they heard a ton of noise coming from the movers.

"Listen, I'm sorry about yelling. I just—" he shrugged "—was surprised to see you."

"Yeah, you said that." Macy put the left earbud in her ear and started to put the second one in. "Next time maybe you can think twice before coming onto my property and yelling at me."

"I'll keep that in mind." He turned and Macy grinned when Jason, who was still hanging over Derek's shoulder, waved at her.

Such a cute kid. Too bad his father is a jerk.

Chapter 4

"Daddy, Macy is pretty," Jason said when Derek set him on his feet but held his hand as they walked back to their house. "Do she have some kids?"

"It's 'Does she have some kids?' and I want you to call her *Ms.* Macy." Derek stopped when they made it back onto his property and bent to his son's level. "And, Jason, I don't want to have to keep talking to you about this girlfriend nonsense or about you asking grown-ups how old they are. Do you understand me?"

Jason kept his head bowed and kicked at the grass beneath his feet.

"Jason, look at me." His son slowly lifted his head and looked at Derek. "Do you understand?"

"Yes," he mumbled.

"Good, because if we have to have this conversation again, there will be consequences." Derek stood to his full height. His son was quickly learning about consequences since he'd had his handheld video game taken away twice last week for misbehaving.

Derek grabbed hold of Jason's hand again, knowing there was a good chance he would take off in a sprint toward the movers. "Oh, and Jason—" his son looked up at him "—you're right. Ms. Macy is pretty, very pretty." They grinned at each other and proceeded to the house.

He still didn't know how he felt about Macy living next door to him. No. Actually, he did know. He hated the idea. She was a distraction he didn't need, especially when she wore shorts that barely covered her butt, showing off just how long her legs really were.

More than once he had caught a couple of movers glancing her way, checking her out. He wondered why she was cutting her own grass anyway. Surely it wouldn't take much effort for her to talk some poor guy into doing it for her.

Jason jerked on his hand, trying to pull away. "Daddy."

"Nope. You're staying with me, at least until we get in the house. I don't want you getting in the way."

"What are they doing?" he asked of the movers.

"They're unloading the truck and taking all of our stuff into the house."

"My toys, too?" Jason asked, his voice pitched higher with excitement.

"Yep, your toys, too." After speaking to one of the movers who was near the truck in the driveway, Derek headed into the house. "Jason, maybe you should hang out in the family room until they're done. I don't want you getting in anyone's way while they're bringing in boxes and furniture. All right?"

"Well, I see you've still got it goin' on with the ladies," Keith said when he strolled into the kitchen, a stupid grin on his face and his key chain spinning around his finger. "I started to go over there and introduce myself to Ms. Short-Shorts, but by the way she was glaring at you, I didn't want any of those daggers to accidentally hit me."

Derek tried to ignore his brother's bark of laughter. He could only imagine what the movers were thinking of the exchange, since he was sure they had witnessed every bit of it. He clearly had overreacted. It was just that when he saw her and the way she was dressed, something inside of him snapped. Thoughts of her had been flitting in and out of his mind for weeks. He didn't want to live next door to her, but in order to fulfill the stipulations Noah had left behind, he needed to stay put for at least a year.

It's going to be a long year.

"It's time, man." Keith interrupted his thoughts.

"Time for what?"

"Time for you to get back out there and start living. Dating."

Derek shook his head. "Keith, don't start. I *have* been living. As a matter of fact, I have a wonderful life that just got better."

"Yeah, you might have more zeros on the numbers in your bank account, but your social life sucks. I know Sam did a number on you, but four years is more than enough time to mourn your marriage." Keith sat at the breakfast bar, across from where Derek was standing. "When was the last time you went on a date? I mean a real date. Not some booty call with a friends-with-benefits type of date."

Derek didn't speak. He hadn't been serious about a woman since his wife walked out on him, ripping out his heart and leaving him with a baby.

"My goal right now is to raise my son and get acclimated to my new job and responsibilities. I don't have time to date." Hell, he wasn't interested in dating seriously. The thought of getting back out there in that scene made his head hurt. Nah, things were fine the way they were.

"Well, you're a fool if you don't get to know your new neighbor. I mean, *really* get to know her." Keith propped his elbows on the counter and rubbed his chin. "You know what? Since you're not interested, maybe I should step to her."

"Now you're talking crazy. Your divorce isn't even final. The last thing you need to be doing is trying to get with anyone." Derek knew his brother was baiting him, but he had no intention of taking it. "Besides, she doesn't seem like the type who would settle for a fling."

"How would you know?"

Yeah, how did he know? He had only spent a little time here and there with her, but even with their small amount of interaction, he could tell she was the marrying type.

"I just know."

"But seriously, dude, don't let your ex ruin the rest

of your life. My marriage might have fallen apart, but that doesn't mean I'm giving up on love."

Derek rolled his eyes. "Good for you."

"And I don't think you should, either. You're always saying that you're doing this or that for Jason, but don't you think he needs a mother?"

"Nope. He has enough women in his life and most important, he has me."

"Mom once said you would make the perfect husband out of all of us. And you know Mom is never wrong." That got a chuckle from Derek. That was his mother's claim to fame—that she was never wrong. "Besides, you're giving your ex too much power. You both were young when you two hooked up. Neither one of you really had a chance to experience life as an adult before marrying and having a kid. Don't base your future on how your past was. Create the future you want." Keith jiggled his keys. "I'll be back in a couple of hours, but think about what I said."

Derek's gaze followed his brother to the door that led out to the garage. A new city, more money than he could ever spend in a lifetime and a beautiful neighbor. Maybe it was time for him to rethink his stance on dating.

Days later, Macy practically glided to the clinic's back door, eagerness bubbling inside her. After operating the facility alone for three years with only a receptionist and a medical assistant, she could barely contain her excitement about bringing on another doctor.

She swung the back door open. "I could kiss you!"

She threw her arms around her longtime friend, Dr. Rachel Thurston, and pulled her close. "I'm so glad to see you. Oh my God, you have no idea how happy I am to see you."

Laughing, Rachel stepped across the threshold. "You just saw me less than a month ago."

"I know, but you weren't a doctor on my staff then." They walked through the hallway that led to the front of the clinic. "I am so hyped to have you here, I feel like dancing on top of the desk."

"Does that mean that with this extra time on your hands, you're going to run out on me and never come back?"

Macy grabbed them both some coffee and they sat in the small space that made up the receptionist's area. Macy swiveled back and forth in the secretary's office chair. For years she'd barely had a day off besides Sunday, and she couldn't remember her last real vacation. Oh yeah, she was super happy to bring on another doctor.

"I won't run away, but I can't wait to see what it feels like to work only four or five days a week instead of seven."

Rachel's brows drew together. "I thought the office was closed on Sundays."

"It is, though lately I have been using Sundays to catch up on paperwork. So that's why I'm happy to see you."

Macy grabbed her tablet from the tidy desk and pulled up her notes of things she needed to go over with Rachel. She had asked her friend to come two hours before the clinic opened in order to fill her in on the day-to-day operations and to play catch-up. A tentative work schedule, clients that would be transferred to her and information about the new medical complex were only a few of the items they needed to discuss.

"Once the medical complex is opened, we'll be moving our operations."

"Are you excited?"

"Very. I have always dreamed of having a facility that houses specialists in more than twenty medical fields under one roof."

"I remember when you first told me about the idea of opening a medical complex, and it looks like you're actually going to pull this off." Rachel put her arm around Macy's shoulders and squeezed. "I'm so proud of you."

"Thank you." Macy smiled. For the first time, her dream seemed reachable.

For the next hour, they went over additional details of what Rachel could expect.

"Okay, I'm all set," Rachel said and placed files back into the cabinet, slamming the drawer closed. "You know, I was sorry to hear about Noah. He was such a great guy and I know how much he meant to you."

"Yeah, I still can't believe he's gone." Macy thought back on the man who had easily fit into her life and became the father she'd never had. "The world has lost a good man."

"I'm glad you had him for as long as you did. My parents died when I was in middle school and I hate they didn't get to see me grow up or see me become a doctor."

Macy stood. "I'm sure they would have been so proud of you."

Rachel shook her head and shivered as if trying to shake off the sadness. "All right, enough of this humdrum stuff. Let's talk about something fun. How's your love life?"

"Ha! Well, this is going to be a short conversation." Macy refilled both their coffee mugs. Her gaze traveled around the colorful reception area and a portion of the waiting room. "This place has pretty much been my life. Between here, my days at the hospital and my volunteer work, there's not much time for a social life." She grabbed her tablet and made sure she wasn't leaving anything behind. "Cindy should be here shortly and will probably kick us out of her space. Let's head to my office."

Rachel followed Macy down the hall. They turned the corner and entered the last room on the right. It wasn't a large area, but Macy appreciated having a place to get away from the riffraff of her days.

"I hear you about the long hours." Rachel sat in the cushioned chair against a nearby wall. "I was putting in sixty, seventy-hour weeks at the hospital. So, when you mentioned the doctor position here, I knew I had to go for it."

"I'm glad you did. I'm sure Trey is going to be happy to have you home a little bit more."

Rachel's beaming smile spoke volumes. Macy only hoped one day she would be able to experience the same type of happiness her friend had in her marriage.

"That's putting it mildly. We'll have been married

a year soon, and he's ready for us to start a family." Rachel sipped from her coffee mug. "So who knows? Maybe we can get started sooner than later." She waggled her eyebrows and they laughed. "Enough about me. Let's talk about you."

Macy wrapped both her hands around her large coffee mug. She was thirty-five, and marriage and having a family weren't far from her mind. She had dated occasionally since her broken engagement four years ago, but being in love was a distant memory. When her ex-fiancé pushed their wedding day back twice in seven months, she'd called the wedding off. Six months later, he was married, and she had recently heard he and his wife were on their second child.

"There's nothing to talk about. Unlike you, my happily-ever-after hasn't shown itself."

"I find that hard to believe." Rachel crossed her legs, dangling her loafer-covered foot. "What about the guy you brought to my birthday party a couple of months ago?" she asked of the man Macy's foster sister Janna had set her up with. "Oh, or what about Dr. *Fine*? You two were going hot and heavy for a while there. What ever happened to him?"

Brandon. Macy really liked him. Tall with broad shoulders and a smile that could melt a glacier, he was not only highly intelligent but he was fun to be around.

"He was a nice guy. It just didn't work out." She set her mug down and traced the rim of it with her finger. "I always felt something was missing between us."

"Something like what?"

Macy gave a slight shrug. "I'm not sure. I guess I

didn't feel fireworks when he kissed me. Don't get me wrong—" she lifted her gaze to her friend "—he's a real sweetheart. It's just that I never experienced that warm and fuzzy feeling whenever he walked into a room." She turned fully in her seat and now faced Rachel. "At least not the way you and my sister Iris look when your men show up. For instance, when Trey walks into a room, your face lights up as if you've just been given a million dollars. Thanks to you and Iris, I recognize the look, but now I want to know how it feels."

Macy's intercom buzzed. "Dr. Carter?"

"Hey, Cindy. What's up?"

"Hi, there. Sorry to bother you, but there is a Derek Logan here to see you."

Macy's heart rate kicked up a notch at the mention of her new, pain-in-the-butt neighbor's name. She couldn't explain her reaction, considering the guy had grated on her nerves a couple of weeks earlier. She could only assume it had something to do with her pitiful sex life.

Rachel lifted an eyebrow. "Soooo, who is Derek Logan?" She placed her feet on the floor and sat forward in her seat. "By your sudden intake of breath and the light sheen of perspiration popping out on your forehead, I'd say he must be someone special."

Macy rolled her eyes at her friend. "Hardly." She pushed the intercom button. "Cindy, would you send him to my office?"

"Of course. I'll escort him back since technically we're not open yet."

"Okay, so talk fast before he gets here," Rachel whispered.

"He's Noah's mentee." Macy pushed wisps of her hair back from her face and tried to put them back into her loose ponytail without any luck. "He's also the architect for the medical complex project."

"And he's a cutie," Rachel said as a statement, not a question, grabbing Macy's attention. "And don't try to deny it. If he weren't, you wouldn't be fixing your hair and smoothing out the invisible wrinkles on your shirt."

A knock sounded on the closed door before Macy could deny her friend's assessment.

"Come in."

Macy's breath hitched when the door swung open and Derek stood in the doorway. *Cutie* wasn't a strong enough word to describe the gorgeous man with eyes that seemed to look right through to her soul.

Good Lord. She hadn't seen him since the day he'd verbally attacked her on her lawn, and today he looked larger than life. His crisp, white dress shirt, designer tie, and tailored pants made him look not only professional but like a sexy boss that would trigger heated conversations at the office watercooler.

Macy swallowed but couldn't seem to get her mouth to work, let alone the rest of her body. She just sat there.

She heard her friend's soft giggle and felt, more than saw, her stand. "Hi, I'm Rachel Thurston. I'm one of the doctors here."

"Nice to meet you, Rachel. Derek Logan." His deep baritone voice washed over Macy, and the moment felt like an out-of-body experience. *What the heck is my problem?* she thought. She didn't even like the guy, yet his presence was making her all tingly inside.

Macy finally shook off her initial shock of seeing him. She stood and wiped her sweaty palms down the sides of her slacks. "What are you doing here?" she asked before she caught herself and realized how snotty she sounded. "I mean… I'm sorry." She stopped and sucked in a deep breath to get her thoughts and words together. "Hi, come in." She waved her hand toward the small sofa. "I wasn't expecting you."

"Apparently," Rachel mumbled loud enough for Macy to hear. "I'm going to get to work." She pointed to the door with her thumb but glanced at Derek, who was still standing near the sofa. "Nice to meet you, Mr. Logan."

"It's Derek." He lifted his hand in a small wave. "And same here. Nice to meet you, as well."

Macy stared after Rachel but turned to Derek when he cleared his throat.

"Sorry to just stop by. At Drew's office, you said I could usually find you here early in the mornings. I figured I'd take a chance on you being here today… on my way into the office." He moved over to the desk where she stood. His scent, both citrusy and woodsy, wrapped around her like a cashmere blanket on a cold winter's night.

She returned to her office chair, unable to understand the butterflies floating around in her stomach.

What was it about this man that jumbled her nerves and seemed to short-circuit her common sense?

Her gaze followed his every move, from his big, strong hands removing a rubber band from around the rolled-up paper in his hands, to picking up items from her desk and setting them on the paper to hold it in place.

He stood back and stuffed his hands into his pants pockets, bringing her attention to how well his tailored trousers fit his lean body.

"I stopped by to show you this—" he pointed to the paper he had just unrolled "—and I wanted to apologize for my behavior the last time we spoke. There's no excuse for my accusatory words and attitude. I hope you can forgive me."

Macy nodded. She could tell when they were keeping vigil over Noah weeks earlier that Derek wasn't a big talker. So she was surprised he was there apologizing.

"It's okay," she finally said and stood. "So what do you have here?"

"These are the plans Noah started for the medical complex."

"What?" Macy moved closer, her shoulder brushing Derek's arm. She stared down at the rough sketches and notes, trying to process what exactly she was looking at. "How? When?"

"From what I understand, he purchased the building about six months ago."

"He never said anything," Macy said just above a whisper, surprised Noah hadn't told her about this. "Why would he have kept this from me?"

"Who knows? You know how Noah was. He marched

to his own beat, doing whatever the heck he wanted to do."

Derek pulled a writing utensil from the black square pencil holder. Hunched over, his hands palms down on the desk, he glanced up at her. It was as if all the air had been sucked out of the room. She swallowed hard as she gazed into the most beautiful brown eyes she'd ever seen on a man. She could easily get lost in them. Why hadn't she noticed the specks of green in his brown irises before?

Her gaze traveled from his eyes down to his kissable lips and what she would give to have just a little taste.

Whoa! Her wanton thoughts slid to a halt. *Okay, this has to stop.*

It had been awhile since she'd been with a man, but it hadn't been that damn long. She didn't even like the guy. Well, she sort of liked him now that he had apologized for his rudeness, but still. Why was she entertaining the thought of kissing him?

The corners of his lips turned upward into a smile and Macy realized he had said something. She gave herself a mental shake.

"I'm sorry. What did you say?"

He chuckled, and the hardy tone sent waves of excitement skittering down her back. *Okay, if I'm getting all goo-goo-eyed and turned on by his laugh, I definitely need to get out more.*

"I said, this is a nice place you have here." He stood upright, and the extra inches he had on her were noticeable. "I had a chance to see some of it when your assistant brought me back. Jason would love how colorful it is and the tons of toys in the waiting room."

Macy smiled at the mention of his son. "You'll have to bring him by sometime to check out the place."

"Well, I do have to find a new pediatrician for him, and according to the way Noah used to talk about you, you're the best."

Heat warmed Macy's cheeks and she returned her attention to the sketches. "So what are your thoughts?"

"Well, I haven't been to the site yet, but I know Noah was brilliant. I figured we can take a look at what he came up with now, and then when we get into the building, we can see what changes you want to make."

"Sounds good." Macy pulled the chair that Rachel had vacated up to the desk and gestured for Derek to have a seat. "So how much time are we looking at for the whole renovation project?" Macy sat in her rolling desk chair and accidentally brushed her knee against his. His closeness was doing wicked things to her peace of mind and if she didn't hurry and get herself together, she was definitely going to embarrass herself.

Derek sat back in his seat and folded his toned arms over his chest. "It's too early to say. I'll need to take a walk through the building. Drew said it was in great condition, but if it doesn't fit what you're looking for, it might take a ton of renovations in order to meet what you have envisioned. We also have to take into consideration the contractor's schedule and when or if they can work this project in. Basically, we need to get into the building and thoroughly check it out before I can give you a rough time frame."

"When can we go in and take a look around?"

Derek thought for a moment, his hand rubbing the scruff on his chin. She had always been attracted to men with mustaches and goatees, and Derek wore his well. Perfectly trimmed and just the right length for both.

"Let's try for Friday?"

"All right." Now that she had another doctor on staff, Macy's schedule would be more flexible.

They talked for a while longer. Derek made notes next to Noah's while he explained some of the architectural symbols Noah had used throughout the rough drawings. Noah had always spoken highly of Derek and now she could see why. Based on the little he had already explained, Noah wasn't the only brilliant one. She could listen to Derek's deep, rhythmic voice talk architecture all day.

Whoa. Macy sat up straight at that last thought. She barely liked him. The last thing she should be thinking about was his voice, or anything else for that matter.

God, give me strength.

Chapter 5

A week later, Derek used a set of spare keys to let himself into the two-story brick building Noah had left to Macy. This was his second time in the future site of the medical complex. Two days earlier, he had walked through to get some preliminary ideas for the complex and take some measurements. Though he respected Macy's dream of opening the health facility, he wondered if she realized how much work she was in for.

Flipping on a few lights, he roamed around the first floor, which was divided into smaller spaces. The building was huge and he was sure it would take at least a year to renovate.

Derek leaned against the counter that must have been used as a customer service or receptionist desk. The facility was located in a decent area near Perimeter Mall, with ample parking and near a bus line; it was in a perfect location. He could honestly say he was looking forward to bringing Macy's dream to fruition. Yet he wasn't looking forward to working so closely with the woman who continued to invade his mind. Not even his ex-wife had affected him the way Macy did.

Derek pushed away from the counter and walked through the narrow hallway toward the back of the building, taking a few mental notes along the way. The ideas he had so far would go great with the layout Noah had started. According to Noah's notes, he had begun working on plans for the complex two months earlier. Derek just didn't know why he hadn't told Macy about the building or that he had already started working on her project. He didn't want to believe his mentor was trying to throw him and Macy together, but the more Derek thought about it, the more he realized that was exactly what Noah had done.

Thinking of Macy, he pulled out his cell phone to see if he had missed a call. He had talked to her earlier that morning to confirm their appointment. Yet here she was, twenty minutes late. He hoped canceling wasn't the norm with her, especially since she had canceled their original appointment the other day. He had a low tolerance for people who didn't respect his time.

Derek returned the cell phone to his pants pocket. *Maybe Louise was right. Maybe I should've offered to pick her up.* Apparently, his assistant knew about Macy's inability to arrive anywhere on time. He'd give her a few more minutes and then he was leaving.

Derek's phone rang as he made his way back to the

front of the building. He dug it out, hoping it wasn't Macy canceling again.

"Hi, this is Derek."

"Derek, I'm sorry to bother you, but I thought you would want to know your two o'clock appointment was rescheduled to three. So you don't have to rush back," Louise said.

"Okay, but so far Macy is a no-show. So I might be…" His voice trailed off when Macy walked in carrying two cups and looking like every man's dream. The sun behind her created a silhouette of her perfectly shaped body. Her thick hair tumbled in large curls over her shoulders and bounced with each long, graceful step she took.

Derek had heard the phrase often enough about a person's mouth going dry, but this was the first time he had ever experienced it. How was it possible that she could get more beautiful each time he saw her? Moments ago, he'd wanted to wring her neck for being late and not respecting his time. Seeing her now had wiped away those thoughts. Each time she walked into a room, it was like letting sunshine into the darkest space.

"Louise, Macy just arrived. I'll make sure I'm there before my three o'clock." After a few more words, he disconnected the call and shoved his phone back into his pocket.

Derek watched as Macy sauntered—no, glided— toward him. He knew one of her sisters was a supermodel. Maybe she had given her tips on how to master a sexy strut. Macy's walk alone would garner a second glance from any man.

He took in her attire. The top three buttons on the sleeveless, light pink blouse she wore were undone and brought just enough attention to her cleavage to let him know she was more than a handful up top. His gaze traveled down her curvaceous body, taking in the way her small waist flared out to shapely hips. Her dark slacks draped over long legs, completing the nice package. He liked that she wasn't skinny, but she was still on the thin side, in his opinion.

He mentally shook himself. *What the hell?* Not only was she his neighbor, but technically she was his client, which meant hands-off. Besides, the last thing he needed right now was to lust after any woman. His life was complicated enough without adding this beautiful distraction.

"Please don't be mad at me. I'm sorry I'm late, but I had a good reason." She handed him one of the cups with Chai Tea written on the side of it. "One of my patient's mothers went into labor while at my clinic, and you can just imagine how crazy things got around there."

Derek saw her lips moving, but her intoxicating fragrance had taken his senses hostage. She smelled of vanilla and roses, and he was tempted to pull her closer for a better whiff.

"Derek." She stood before him with her hand on her hip and a frown on her lovely face. "Say something."

He hesitated, trying to get his body under control. Her presence had an effect on him that he hadn't experienced in a while, and now was definitely not a good time.

"You're late." He turned and headed to the back of the building, ignoring her frustrated growl.

"You can at least thank me for the drink." She hurried behind him, her short heels clicking against the ceramic tile. "Can't you just once say something nice to me without giving me a frown *or* your *back*?"

Derek slowed his steps and blew out a breath. He stopped in the middle of the hallway and took a sip from the cup, eyeing her over the rim. "How'd you know I drink chai tea?"

"When we were at the hospital with Noah, I noticed you weren't a coffee drinker, only soda and hot tea." She shrugged. "Since soda isn't good for you, I opted for tea. I guess I got lucky with getting chai."

Derek didn't know what to say. The fact she had noticed his drinks of choice surprised him. Back then, most days they had seen each other only in passing, choosing not to spend time in Noah's room together.

"Thanks." He turned and resumed walking. "Let's start back here."

"Fine." She threw her free arm up and let it drop down, slapping against her thigh. "See if I ever do anything nice for you again," she mumbled.

For the next hour and a half, they roamed around both the first and second floors of the building. Derek jotted down notes and a few sketches as Macy shared her vision for the medical complex. He appreciated her passion for wanting to create a facility that catered to all walks of people.

"Well, I think I have enough to get started." Derek backtracked and turned off lights that were turned on.

"I'll come up with some preliminary sketches for you and we'll go back and forth a couple of times until we get just what you want."

"Sounds good." Macy slipped on her shades as they stepped out into the heat. Atlanta clearly earned its nickname—Hotlanta. "Derek, I really appreciate you doing this for me. I know Noah kinda roped you into this project, but I'm glad I get to work with you. He spoke highly of your skills, and now I get to witness them firsthand."

"No problem. I'm glad I can help."

"I would imagine you're crazy busy these days, trying to get situated in your new role as owner and CEO of Price. And you're taking care of your little boy."

To say the past few weeks had been like something out of a dream would be an understatement. He literally became a millionaire overnight, then picked up his life and moved it hundreds of miles from his family.

"Let's just say this is an interesting season in my life." He slipped on his shades as they walked to their cars. Despite the way they'd started, he found himself enjoying Macy's company and, surprisingly, hated their time together coming to an end. He walked her to her BMW, parked in front of his vehicle. "Do you have time for some lunch?"

Macy leaned against her car, tilted her shades down and let them perch at the end of her nose. Looking over the rim of them, she said, "You…want to go to lunch with me?"

Of course, she would be shocked. He had done nothing to show her that he actually liked her. While visiting Noah at the hospital, he'd tried to stay clear of her. And when he found out she was his next-door neighbor, he'd practically jumped down her throat, accusing her of being in cahoots with Noah in some type of matchmaking scheme. So his offer of lunch probably did catch her off guard.

"Look, I know we...well, I know I have made things a little awkward between us. Why don't we start over?" He stretched out his hand. "Hi, I'm Derek Logan. It's nice to meet you."

She pushed her sunglasses up on her nose and grinned. "Nice to meet you, Derek. I'm Macy Carter." Still smiling, she shook his hand.

"Would you give me the pleasure of having lunch with me?"

"Sure, but can we drop the formal stuff? You're scaring me." She laughed and he joined in. Derek had to admit it felt good to laugh, something he didn't do often enough.

Since she was more familiar with the area, he followed her to a nearby restaurant. Derek couldn't remember the last time he had taken a woman out. He had initially scoffed at Keith's suggestion about dating, but maybe it wouldn't hurt to have lunch or dinner with a female companion occasionally.

Small talk flowed freely between them as they walked from the parking lot to the building. He opened the door to the restaurant and with his hand at the small of Macy's back, guided her in. The heat that charged up his arm was starting to become a norm whenever he touched her. The feeling was so intense he wondered if she felt it, as well.

Seated at a booth near the back of the establishment, Derek glanced around the intimate space as Macy gave him a little history on the neighborhood. Based on their ongoing conversation earlier, he wasn't surprised she knew so much about the area.

"Are you two ready to order?" the server asked.

"Are you ready?" Derek asked Macy.

"Yes, actually, I am. I'll have the Swiss and turkey panini." Macy's soft words floated through the air. She traced her finger along her water glass, catching the perspiration as she continued to study the menu. She looked up and smiled at the server. "Instead of the salad, may I have coleslaw?"

"Of course." The server turned to Derek. "And for you?"

Derek had been so busy staring at Macy, he hadn't really narrowed down his choices. After another quick glance at the entrées, he said, "I'll have the beef tenderloin and pasta salad." He handed his menu to the server. "Could you also bring me a Coke?"

A little while later, the server returned with their meals.

"So how has everything been going?" Macy asked between bites. "You've been in town for a while. Does it feel like home yet?"

"We're getting there. It helps that my brother hasn't started his new job yet. Once he's working, I'm going to have to find a preschool program, as well as a babysitter for Jason."

"I'm sure I can come up with a short list of programs for you. Also my niece, Tania, is on summer break. She'll be starting at Spelman this fall, but I'm sure she wouldn't mind watching Jason for you sometime."

"That would be great." If things worked out with Macy's niece, it would be one thing he could scratch off his to-do list. "Is it possible for me to meet her sometime in the next couple of days?"

"I'm sure that won't be a problem. I'll call her this evening."

"Perfect."

"So tell me something about yourself. I've met your brother Keith. Do you have any more siblings?" she asked. Derek wasn't usually a big talker outside of his family or a business setting, so he appreciated how Macy kept the conversation going.

"I have a total of four brothers, three older and one younger."

Macy's fork stopped midair and her mouth dropped open. "There are five of you?" He laughed at her facial expression. "Any sisters?"

He shook his head. "Nope, but not from lack of trying. Once my youngest brother Craig was born, I think my parents gave up on the idea of having a daughter. Or it could be they stopped because my father was killed in Desert Storm when I was in high school."

"Oh, Derek, I'm so sorry."

He shrugged. "It was a long time ago." He signaled for the server. "Can we get a few more napkins?" he asked when she came over.

"Of course. I'll be right back with some."

"So you mentioned a niece, Tania. How many siblings do you have? Any more nieces or nephews?"

"As a matter of fact, one of my sisters, Iris, is expecting twins in a few months."

"Oh, wow, congratulations."

A huge grin spread across her lips. "Thank you. We're all pretty excited."

"Siblings?"

"Well, actually, I grew up in foster care. My two foster sisters, Iris and Janna, might not be blood related, but we're closer than most biological siblings. And they drive me nuts sometimes, like real sisters." The warmth in her beautiful brown eyes entranced him. If he kept staring into them, he was definitely going to do something that was sure to get him slapped—like kiss her.

"I'm sure they don't get on your nerves as much as brothers would. I'm always trying to give mine away." They laughed and exchanged stories of growing up with siblings. The conversation turned more serious when Macy shared some of the lows of being in foster care, like being bounced from house to house for the first few years of her life. It wasn't until she ended up with Mama Adel that she'd felt as if she was home.

When Derek talked about his family, it made him miss them that much more. His mother and two of his brothers lived in Columbus and Craig was still in Cincinnati. But when Derek had lived in Ohio, they'd made it a point to get together often.

"You've had a lot of changes in your life lately," Macy said.

Derek stretched his arm across the back of the booth

he was sitting in and tried to get comfortable. Calling the way his life had been turned upside down and becoming an instant millionaire "changes" was an understatement.

"Things have been interesting but good. I knew it would take a while to get used to the house and a new city, but I think the biggest challenge for me is at work."

"How so?"

"I've been self-employed and a stay-at-home dad for the past three years, deciding to start my own business when Jason was one." He toyed with the white linen napkin near his glass of water. "It's been years since I've had to go into an office for meeting after meeting, and don't even get me started on having direct reports again. But I have to say one thing. I know why Noah talked about Louise all the time. The woman is *amazing.*"

Macy nodded, and the huge smile that graced her lips snagged his attention. Enraptured by how her whole face lit up in the process, his gaze steadied on her full, ruby-red lips until he realized he was staring.

Damn. Now he remembered why he was trying to keep his distance from her. There was something about her that sent his mind in every direction other than where it should be.

"Noah used to always joke that Louise was the real boss at Price, keeping him and everyone else in line. I'm glad she's still there and helping you get settled."

"I don't know what I would do without her. Actually, I don't know what I would do without any of them.

Noah left behind an impressive team, and they have all stepped in to help me in one way or another."

She wiped her mouth and placed the napkin back in her lap. "Noah thought of them as family."

Derek didn't miss the sadness that suddenly flashed in her eyes. He, too, had those moments when thoughts of Noah brought back happier times, but then he'd think about how he was no longer there.

Her expression changed and the sadness in her eyes was gone as fast as it had appeared.

"If you don't mind me asking, where's Jason's mother?"

Derek set his fork down, jarred by the new direction of their conversation. This was one question he hadn't expected. He might've been enjoying their time together and could see them one day being friends, but discussing his ex was off-limits.

"We divorced a few years ago." Maybe one day he would share the whole story with her, but not today. "What time do you have to be back at the clinic?" He changed the subject. If he planned to get back into the dating scene, at some point he would have to come to grips with what his ex-wife had done. Otherwise, he'd never be able to let another woman get close to him.

Macy glanced at her cell phone lying on the table. "My next appointment is in thirty minutes."

"Well, I guess we'd better eat up."

Macy waved him off. "No rush. I'm only fifteen minutes away. So there's plenty of time."

With that attitude, it was no wonder she had been

late. "So, tell me, are you always late for meetings and appointments?"

She stopped eating and glared at him. "Are you always so impatient, standoffish and irritating?"

Derek hesitated and then burst out laughing. He sat back in his seat and she went back to eating, but not before he saw the small quiver of a smile on her tempting lips. He could honestly say he had never met anyone like her. Beautiful, smart and said what was on her mind. A woman after his own heart.

"That's what you think of me, huh?"

Macy finished chewing before she spoke. "Well… what else am I supposed to think? When I first met you at the hospital, you barely said two words to me. Then you find out I live next door to you and you go ballistic, charging at me like I was an enemy from outer space."

"Macy."

"I'm not finished yet." She set down her fork and wiped her mouth. It was time for someone to knock him down a peg or two. She might as well be the one to do it. "And what about the way you glared at me when I showed up late for our meeting today? You didn't bother asking me why I was late. All you did was treat me like crap."

"Macy."

"I had back-to-back patients this morning and then one of the parents went into labor. I couldn't just very well leave."

"I'm sorry." He grabbed hold of her hand and gave it a tug, immediately shutting her up. As before, his touch sent a bolt of electricity up her arm and through her body. No man had ever stirred that type of reaction in her, and she wasn't sure what it was about Derek that made her body tingle all over. She could blame it on sexual deprivation. Yet there had been other times in her life that she had gone without for just as long. Her body had never reacted this way. She didn't want to be attracted to him. He clearly had some baggage that made him behave like a caveman. Then again, he proved he could be nice when he wanted to be.

She slid her hand from his grasp, enjoying his touch a little too much. "Apology accepted."

She gazed into his alluring eyes and quickly looked away. The man oozed sex appeal. He had broad shoulders, was meticulously dressed and had eyes so dark and intense, his gaze sent chill bumps down her arms. Having lunch with him stoked the fire that had started building within her the first time they'd met. The flames were growing hotter by the minute.

The handsome Derek Logan was definitely getting under her skin. To see him standing in the hallway when she arrived at the future medical complex, in his crisp light blue dress shirt with the sleeves rolled up to the middle of his forearms, had made her want to run her hands down his chest and feel the hard planes of his body beneath her touch. He looked sexier than he ever had before.

Yeah, it had to be sexual deprivation. Lust shot through her each time he looked at her. The juncture between her thighs throbbed at the sound of his voice, especially when he talked architecture or released that hearty laugh of his.

Even his brooding attitude did nothing to decrease her attraction to him. It didn't make sense. When he had guided her into the restaurant, his large hand on her back, he'd had her heart pounding so fast she thought it would beat right out of her chest.

"Macy. Macy?"

Derek's deep voice brought her back to the present. Her gaze met his concerned one.

"You zoned out on me. You okay?"

"Oh yeah. Yeah, I'm fine." She tried to laugh it off, hoping he didn't think she was some type of flake, staring at him the way she was.

They talked more about family, and she was starting to see a different side of him throughout lunch. Who knew he had a sense of humor? At this rate, maybe future meetings with him wouldn't be too bad.

Her phone beeped, letting her know she had just enough time to get back to the clinic.

"Well, that's my cue." She tossed her napkin onto the table and gathered her bag. "I need to get back, but thanks for lunch. It's been nice getting to know you. You're not the ogre I once thought you to be."

He laughed and glanced at the check before pulling out his wallet. "Well, I'm glad I'm not as bad as you originally thought. Hopefully, as time goes on, you'll see I'm an all-right kind of guy."

"Yeah, well, we'll see."

Chapter 6

Derek strolled through the impressive lobby of Price Architecture, greeting people along the way. If he had any doubt of the company's success, just walking through the unique asymmetrical building brought it home. With glass, chrome and an art deco feel to the environment, it truly was a work of art. The firm and its team of administrators, architects and engineers occupied the top four floors of the twenty-story building. They rented out the rest of the floors to a variety of companies, from law offices to virtual assistants.

"Good morning, Mr. Logan," the security guard at the customer service desk greeted him.

"Morning, Casey, and please call me Derek," he said as he walked toward the elevators.

The guard smiled and nodded. "Will do, sir."

Derek chuckled. Casey was the same age as him and hearing the guy refer to him as "sir" was too weird. That was one thing about the South he didn't think he'd ever get used to.

Derek took the all-glass elevator up to the twentieth floor and did a mental catalog of his day. He had several one-on-one meetings with a couple of his top people, and then he and Macy were meeting. Just thinking about his beautiful neighbor sent heat rushing through his body. He hated the way he had verbally attacked her in her yard weeks ago, but it was something about her that seemed to bring out sides of him that otherwise rarely made an appearance.

"Good morning, Louise," Derek said when he walked into the front office, his assistant behind her desk.

Louise glanced up and smiled. "Morning, Derek. I placed the files that you'll need for the meeting with Tom and Robert on your desk. Oh, and Tom sent up the financial information you requested. He wasn't sure if you two would have time to go over it this morning but wanted you to have it just in case."

"Thanks, I'm hoping we'll be able to get to that this morning."

The CFO and the COO had welcomed him to the team as if they'd known him forever. Granted, Derek had met them many years ago during his internship, but he hadn't seen either of them in years.

Derek walked into his office, which was twice the size of the studio apartment he'd had in college. He set his briefcase on top of the huge cherrywood desk that once belonged to Noah. His mentor's presence still filled the room.

Louise had asked Derek a series of questions when he had first started regarding how he wanted his office equipped. With those few answers, she had pegged him and his style perfectly. The brown leather sofa in the far corner of the room wasn't something he had requested, but it fit flawlessly into the space. His number one requirement for his office was a drafting table. He had gotten a little emotional when he walked in that first day and saw Noah's table set up near the desk. Memories of how they used to stand over it, drawing up plans, came rushing back to him.

Derek turned to the window behind his desk and stared out onto Peachtree Street, awed by the chain of events that had become his new life. Some days he still had trouble believing the role he was now playing. *CEO.* He was responsible for the overall operations of the organization and reported to the board of directors. Prior to working as a freelancer and becoming a stay-at-home dad, he had been a mid-manager at an architectural firm in Cincinnati. Now, not only was he the CEO, he was also the president and chairman of Price Architecture.

He sat behind the desk and pulled up his calendar on the computer. Time to get the day started. Seeing Macy's name on his schedule for later that afternoon, he pulled out the file for her project. He had some good ideas already in the works, and if he could get her to quit making changes, they might be able to finish the first draft of the prints.

A small smile spread across his lips and he shook his head. If only he could get her to be on time for at least one of their meetings, he just might be able to work with her for the duration of the project.

Macy rushed through the hospital halls toward Amber's room, greeting a few staff along the way. Her young patient, diagnosed with leukemia nine months earlier, had been showing improvement over the past couple of months. Macy thought for sure she was going to beat this awful disease. Unfortunately, pneumonia was a complication that could definitely set back any progress Amber had made.

Macy shook her head. *Only positive thoughts. Only positive thoughts.*

"Oh, thank God," Amber's mother said as she walked toward Macy. "Dr. Carter, she is so weak and she's been asking for you. Thanks so much for coming."

"Of course." Macy wrapped her arm around the woman's shoulders and they walked to Amber's room together. Dr. Stanley exited the room before they reached it.

"How is she?"

He glanced at Amber's mother before returning his attention to Macy. "She's hanging in there, but—"

"Oh God," Amber's mother said, and Macy tightened her hold around her. Apparently, she saw the same sadness in the doctor's eyes that Macy had seen. The prognosis wasn't good.

"Can I go in and see her?" Macy asked, and the doctor nodded.

She pushed open the hospital room door and moved to the side of Amber's bed. At six years old, Amber was small for her age, but she looked even smaller in the bed and against the white sheets.

"Amber." Macy lifted the little girl's hand. "Sweetheart, can you hear me?"

Macy's heart stuttered when Amber slowly lifted her lids and dull gray eyes stared up at her.

She had lost a patient to cancer a few years ago, and though she knew everyone would one day die, it wasn't something she handled well, especially when that someone was a child. She had dedicated her life to caring for children and it broke her heart whenever she lost one.

A small smile lifted the corner of Amber's pale pink lips and no words escaped Macy. All she could do at the moment was send up a prayer that everything would work out for Amber.

She has to be okay.

"Hi, Dr. Carter." Amber's hoarse whisper sent chill bumps up Macy's arm as she fought to keep her tears at bay. No matter how many of her patients ended up with life-threatening diseases, it never got any easier maintaining hope that they would pull through.

"Hi, sweetheart."

She caressed Amber's cheek with the back of her fingers. She didn't have a daughter of her own, but lately that was all she could think about—getting married and having a family. The only thing was, if she ever had to endure what Amber's parents had been going through, Macy knew it would kill her.

Thirty minutes later, after consulting with Amber's doctor, Macy hung out with Amber and her mother until the little girl fell asleep. Her father, stationed overseas, was expected back in the States later that day. Macy found solace in knowing the staff was doing everything it could for Amber, though her health was quickly declining.

Macy promised Amber's mother she would return after her meeting. She had an appointment with Derek in twenty minutes to go over the latest plans he had drawn up, and the last thing she wanted to do was be late. Besides, she was looking forward to seeing him. They had met twice since the day they had lunch together. So far she was glad she hadn't written him off. Though she didn't like the way Noah had thrown them together, she could honestly say she liked Derek and was glad they were becoming friends.

Now, here she was sitting in a long line with other drivers who were trying to exit the parking lot.

"Come on, people," she said into the quietness of the car. She'd been sitting for twenty minutes and was reluctantly getting ready to call Derek when her pager went off.

Groaning, she stole a quick glance at it: *911*.

Her heart dropped. She hated when her service sent her 911 messages, knowing the news wouldn't be good. Instead of calling Derek, she called the hospital.

"Hi, this is Dr. Carter."

Tears pricked behind her eyes as she sat stunned, listening to the call. *Oh, Amber.* Knowing the little girl wasn't doing well only minutes ago still hadn't prepared her for this moment.

Macy swiped at a few tears that slipped through and pulled out of line. She couldn't leave. There was no way she could abandon Amber's mother right now. If she was asking herself why, she knew she couldn't begin to know what that child's mother was going through.

She dried her face and took a few cleansing breaths. *Time to put on a brave front.*

An hour later, Macy climbed back into her car and stared out the front window, her hands tightly gripping the steering wheel. She knew as well as anyone that there was a thin line between life and death, but lately she'd been feeling overwhelmed with the latter. First Noah and now Amber. Noah had assured her he was ready for what God had in store for him and was excited about seeing his late wife on the other side, as he had put it. But Amber, she was just a baby.

On one hand, Macy appreciated every breath she'd been given, but on the other hand, she would have gladly given Amber her remaining breaths if it could have saved her life. Too bad it didn't work like that. She felt so helpless. She had committed her life to help save others, but today it didn't seem to be enough.

The downpour of rain slamming against her car fit her mood. Depleted of energy, she just wanted to go home, crawl into her bed and sleep for a month. She rested her head on the steering wheel and closed her eyes. She loved being a doctor, but it was days like today that made her wonder if she should consider a different line of work.

Her cell phone beeped again. According to its various tones over the past hour, she had received several calls and just as many text messages. Not in the mood to speak to anyone, she remained where she was but then thought better of not checking her messages.

She dug the phone out of the side pocket of her bag and glanced at the screen.

Derek.

Derek paced in front of his drafting table and rubbed the back of his neck. This was the third time that Macy was late for one of their appointments and her last chance to have him work on her project. His time was too valuable to waste on someone who clearly didn't respect it.

He couldn't understand it. How could someone who was so intelligent and pulled together be consistently inconsiderate? Had it not been for the stipulations in Noah's will, he would have already assigned a different architect to Macy. He didn't have the patience or the time to work with someone who wasn't serious about getting her project done, regardless of his attraction to her.

His cell phone rang from where it sat on the desk. Not bothering to look at the screen, thinking it was Macy, he picked it up and answered right away.

"Hello," he growled, his patience spent.

"Well, hello to you, too, little brother," Keith said, the humor in his voice coming through loud and clear.

"What's got you riled up? Oh no, wait. Let me guess. It's that gorgeous neighbor of ours, right?"

Derek didn't bother answering the question. Instead, he asked, "How's my son doing?"

"He's fine, but he says Tania is a better babysitter than I am." Keith laughed, not offended in the least bit by Jason's crush on her. "He's planning to ask you if she can watch him from now on."

Derek smiled. He couldn't blame his son's choice in babysitters. Tania always came with projects for them to do, as well as microwave popcorn, another one of Jason's favorites.

"So, why are you calling?"

"Just wondering when you were planning to head home. If you're going to be a while, I was thinking of taking Lil' Man out for pizza."

Derek glanced at his watch. "Actually, I should be…" His voice trailed off when he heard the door to the outer office open. Most of his team had left for the day, and Louise had gone home an hour earlier. Still holding his cell to his ear, he took a few steps toward the door but stopped. Macy stood in the doorway. Not only was she soaked from the downpour outside, she looked as if she'd been through hell.

"Uh, Keith, let me call you back. As a matter of fact, maybe you should proceed with your plans with Jason." Derek disconnected the call and laid his cell phone on the desk, not taking his gaze from Macy.

Without speaking, she blew out a breath and ran her hand over her long, limp hair. Her shoulders hung low as if she carried the weight of the world on her back. Seconds passed and she still didn't say a word.

Derek sat on the edge of his desk and folded his arms across his chest. He perused her attire, taking in the wet, pink blouse plastered to her upper body, emphasizing her voluptuous breasts. It had been raining for the past half hour and she clearly had gotten caught in it. His gaze went lower to where her wet pants stuck to her firm thighs. And even lower to where she now stood in a small puddle of water on the floor, wearing sandals that showed pretty feet with pink polish on her toes.

Derek's gaze traveled back up to her face. Once again, his body betrayed him as he zoned in on her enticing lips and imagined what it would be like to kiss her. Despite the dark smudges under her eyes, as if she hadn't been sleeping well, she was still one of the most beautiful women he'd ever met.

He rubbed his eyes and exhaled a loud breath. He was never going to find out whether or not her lips were as soft as they appeared. Whatever attraction he had for Macy was going to stop there; it was just attraction. They could be friends, but it couldn't go any further. Or at least that's what he kept telling himself. He had too much going on in his life to even consider getting involved with someone, especially her. Besides, she lived next door and he never got involved with anyone who lived within walking distance of him. If the relationship didn't work out, he didn't want to risk running into the person on a daily basis.

"I don't think this is going to work, Macy," he said

finally. "You're two hours late. Monday, I'll assign a different archi—"

"Derek, I..." Her voice cracked and her face contorted as if she was in pain. She cupped her hand over her mouth and smothered a sob as tears rolled down her face.

What the hell? Surely she couldn't be that broken up about him assigning someone else to her project. No, something else was going on.

Derek pushed away from his desk. "What happened?" She didn't appear to be hurt, but he didn't want to assume. He wrapped his arms around her and pulled her close. "Are you okay?" he asked close to her ear; her intoxicating fragrance drifted up to his nostrils and he breathed in deep. Rubbing her back, he realized how dumb his question sounded. Clearly, she wasn't okay.

He pulled her even closer as her sobs grew louder, ignoring the fact that she was getting his dress shirt wet. Placing a kiss against her temple, he berated himself for loving the way she felt in his arms.

Her sobs eventually quieted and she frantically wiped the tears from her face. Derek stood back and shoved his hands into his pockets.

"Tell me what's going on."

"I'm so sorry for this." She dug through her purse and pulled out a small pack of tissues. "And I'm sorry I missed our meeting. It's just..." She dabbed at her eyes, seeming to struggle with forming her words.

"It's just what?" Derek asked, thinking it had to be something pretty bad to make her break down the way she had. She came across as a pillar of strength, the person that people went to when they had a problem. Now she looked so vulnerable.

"One of my patients died a couple of hours ago." She tossed her tissue into the trash can near the drafting table and pulled another from the small pack in her hand. "I don't usually break down like this when I lose a patient, but she wasn't just any patient. This little girl was six years old and…and she was very special to me."

"I'm so sorry, Macy."

He gently held her elbow and guided her over to the seating area of his office, helping her to one of the upholstered chairs while he took the other. A heavy weight settled around Derek's heart. His son would be five soon, and the thought of going through anything like what the little girl's parents were dealing with scared Derek to death. He couldn't imagine a life without Jason.

His heart went out to the child's parents…and to Macy. He wasn't the squirmy type when it came to seeing blood or anything like that, but he didn't know how doctors did it day in and day out. Granted, they saved many lives, but he had no idea how they dealt with so much loss.

"Amber had been diagnosed with leukemia months ago. Until recently, we thought she could beat it. I wanted her to beat it." She sobbed. "She got pneumonia and today…"

When Macy stood suddenly, Derek stood, as well.

"I'm sorry to lay this all on you. And again, I'm

sorry about missing our appointment. I know you have a lot going on these days." Her voice sounded as if she was going to break down again. "Maybe you should assign me to someone else."

"Wait." Derek gently grabbed her arm before she stepped out of his office. "I can't let you leave like this." She started crying again. Derek wondered if something else was going on with her. It hadn't been long ago that she'd lost Noah, and Derek didn't know if she had lost any other patients in between then and now.

He held her at arm's length. Her head was down; lifting her chin with the tip of his finger, he forced her to look at him. His heart clenched inside his chest. He couldn't stand to see her like this. She had the prettiest brown eyes he had ever stared into, and right now they were some of the saddest ones he'd ever stared into.

He stepped closer and cupped her face; the pads of his thumbs wiped at her tears. When his gaze settled on her plump lips, it was as if a magnetic force was at work between them.

Leaning forward, he lowered his head and touched his lips to hers. At first, the kiss was a gentle peck, but he wanted more. He moved one of his hands to her waist and the other to the back of her neck, deepening the kiss. Her soft moans spurred him on and he savored her sweetness.

Derek, surprised by her eager response, knew if he didn't stop kissing her right then, he wouldn't be able to stop. He abruptly pulled his mouth from hers but didn't let her go. Instead, he rested his forehead against hers, trying to catch his breath. He didn't regret the kiss, but part of him felt as if he should apologize, especially since she wasn't herself tonight. But if one kiss ignited a flame within him the way that one did, he had no doubt they would spontaneously combust if they ever hit the sheets together.

Take care of her. Noah's deathbed request invaded Derek's thoughts. Macy came across as very strong and independent, but maybe his mentor knew something Derek didn't.

Derek lifted his head and caressed her soft cheek. "I'll take you home so you can get out of those wet clothes."

"Thank you, but I drove my car."

"Leave it." He grabbed his keys and cell phone. "I don't think it's a good idea for you to drive tonight."

Chapter 7

Macy stared out the passenger window of Derek's car and watched as the city went by in a blur. Her fingers went to her lips as she thought about the kiss she and Derek had shared in his office. Nothing could have prepared her for the heat that consumed her when his mouth touched hers. How had she gone from telling him about Amber to being wrapped in his arms, her tongue tangling with his?

Her body turned hot with the memory of his lips against hers, his strong arms cradling her body. No one had ever kissed her so thoroughly, leaving her lusting for more. The dull ache between her thighs hadn't been awakened in a long time, and it was all because of an impromptu kiss. But then he'd pulled away just as quickly.

She dropped her hand to her lap and laid her head against the headrest, closing her eyes. She didn't want to read too much into their intense lip-lock, but she couldn't help it. She'd be lying if she said that she hadn't wanted that kiss.

"You okay?" Derek's baritone voice seemed even deeper than usual. Chill bumps crawled up her arms that weren't caused by the blast of air from the air conditioner.

"I'm fine." She sat up and stole a glance at him, shadows from the streetlights casting a romantic glow inside the car. The velvety sounds of Alex Bugnon stroking his ivory keys played through the car speakers, adding to the smooth ride. "Thanks for driving me. I'm sure I could have gotten myself home, but I appreciate you offering."

"Not a problem. It's not like it's out of my way or anything." He turned to her, a slight smile bringing her attention to those amazing lips. "Besides—" he returned his attention to the road "—you weren't in any condition to drive."

She knew he was right. "I'm not sure what happened. Granted, losing a patient is never easy, but I can't ever remember feeling this…this helpless and sad. I thought for sure Amber had made a turn for the better, and then *poof.*" She snapped her fingers. "She's gone. And all I can think about is her poor parents. Her father is in the military. He was able to take an emergency leave a few months ago, but when Amber started making improvements, he returned to duty. He was expected back today."

Derek gripped the steering wheel tighter. "I can't even imagine going through something like that with Jason. He means everything to me. How does someone move on from losing a child?"

Macy shook her head. "I don't know. And God knows, I hope I never have to find out." She had wanted children for as long as she could remember, but her window of opportunity was slowly closing.

"Have you ever thought about having children?" Derek asked out of nowhere.

Macy stared at his profile before turning to the passenger window. "I think about it all the time. I would love to have at least three, but at my age, the chances of that are pretty slim, especially since I'd prefer to be married first. I know too many single parents out there trying to do it on their own, and that's not what I want." The moment the words left her mouth, she realized what she had said. "I'm not saying it's impossible to raise children on my own. I'm just—"

"Don't worry. I understand what you're saying. Trust me, I never thought I'd be a single parent." He put his blinker on and changed lanes. Macy had hoped he would say more about how he came to be one but he didn't.

"Are you still in contact with Jason's mother?" She really didn't have a right to ask, but curiosity got the best of her. If he didn't want her to know, he could always tell her to mind her own business.

"No. My ex-wife walked out on us when Jason was six months old, claiming she couldn't handle being a wife and mother. As far as I'm concerned, she doesn't exist anymore."

* * *

Derek gripped the steering wheel tighter. Each time he thought about his ex, it felt as if he was being stabbed in the heart with a knife over and over again. He was no longer in love with her, but the pain she had caused when she walked out was something he had forgiven, but he would never forget.

"I am so sorry." Macy placed her hand on his thigh and that usual electric charge he felt whenever they touched stormed through his body. Unlike previous times, she didn't snatch her hand away. "That had to be devastating."

He released a noisy sigh and didn't speak right away. Yet there was something about Macy that made him want to tell her about that time in his life. A time he rarely discussed with anyone. Maybe it was her compassion, which he had witnessed on more than one occasion. Or it could be he felt he could trust her.

"That was one of the worst days of my life," he mumbled, debating just how much he wanted to share. "We had dated for a couple of years, made all types of plans of how perfect our life would be. We had talked about having three children—" Derek glanced at Macy "—but three or four months before Jason was born, I started noticing some changes in her. She was withdrawn, stayed out late with some of her friends, and there was one time, when she was eight months pregnant, when she stayed out all night." His voice hitched and Macy ran her hand up and down his thigh, as if that would relax him. If anything, the movement of her hand was driving him crazy.

"What happened when she showed up?" Macy's question was spoken so softly, but Derek didn't miss the concern he heard in her words.

"She gave some excuse about time getting away from her and that she had stayed the night with one of her friends." Anger reared its wicked head as the words took him back to that morning. *Livid* wasn't a strong enough word to describe what he'd felt for his wife that day.

"Is she still in Jason's life?"

Derek shook his head. "I haven't seen or heard from her since our divorce became final. She showed up for the hearing and that was the last I saw of her."

Except for the jazz pianist playing low through the speakers, silence fell between them. Derek hadn't planned to share that much with Macy, especially knowing she had just lost a patient. She didn't need to hear about his baggage.

"I'm so sorry that happened to you and Jason, but from what I know of your son, I think you're doing an amazing job with him." She finally removed her hand, and he released the breath he hadn't realized he was holding.

"Thanks. It was a long time ago. I'm just glad Jason came out healthy."

"Did you ever find out what was going on with her?"

Derek thought about the question for a moment. At the time, he had thought his ex was seeing someone else, but if she was, she hid it well. After her disappearing act, a PI friend did surveillance for him and followed her until Jason was born. "To this day, I'm not really sure what was going on. A couple of weeks after that incident, Jason was born and she seemed fine. One of my fears during her weird stage was that she was on drugs or something, but nothing was found in her system. Jason was born perfectly healthy and to this day he's rarely been sick."

"Well, that's good."

Derek exited the highway and drove in the direction of both their homes. "I shouldn't have been surprised by my ex's behavior," he said without Macy prompting, wanting to share the rest of it. "Her mother had abandoned her family, as well."

Macy gasped and Derek glanced her way, noticing how her hand was resting on her chest. He hated seeing pity in her eyes, but he wasn't sure if the look was for him or his ex's situation.

"So sad," Macy finally said.

"Yeah." Derek made a right turn that put them about ten minutes outside their neighborhood. "That's why I was surprised that she left. Prior to getting married, she had often said that she would never leave her family the way her mother had. I guess maybe I shouldn't have been surprised history repeated itself."

"No." Macy started to speak, and Derek looked in her direction when she didn't say anything further.

"No, what?"

"History doesn't always repeat itself," she said with such conviction that Derek slowed the SUV down. "I refuse to believe that. My mother abandoned me like it was the easiest thing in the world to do. But I know without a doubt I would never, ever abandon my husband or my child. Never."

Derek didn't speak. He wasn't sure what to say. He had heard that before, yet here he was raising his son alone. Sure, Macy was nothing like his ex, from what he could tell, but he couldn't say yet if she was or wasn't the type of person to leave her family.

He pulled into her circular driveway and shut off the car. She hadn't said anything for the past few minutes and for a while he thought maybe she had fallen asleep. Studying her now, she looked exhausted and he regretted saying anything about his ex.

"Listen, I'm sorry about…everything. Amber, the discussion about my ex, all of it. I definitely didn't mean to make your evening even more depressing."

She shook her head. "No, I'm sorry about my outburst." She turned in her seat to face him, the sadness in her eyes making his chest tighten. "I just didn't want you to think children who have been abandoned by their parents always turn around and do the same thing. I want my own family so bad, I can't even imagine walking away from something I have been waiting so long for." She quickly swiped at a single tear. "Please don't think all women are like that."

Derek reached out and cupped her cheek before he could stop himself. He didn't have too much faith in women these days, but listening to Macy's heartfelt plea was affecting him in a way he wasn't familiar with.

More tears slid down her face and he caught a few, wiping them away with his thumb. Instead of saying anything, he leaned in and touched his lips to hers. He hadn't planned to kiss her again, but...

He moved his mouth over hers and devoured its softness. There was just something about this woman... Sweet. Precious. Enticing. Derek lifted his hand and caressed her cheek as their kiss grew more intense. He couldn't get enough of her. He had wanted to taste her lips from the moment he met her, and tonight he had tasted her twice. That would never be enough. However, getting involved with Macy could be trouble. She wanted marriage and kids. He didn't.

Derek moved his mouth from hers but didn't move his hand from her cheek. Staring into her eyes, he knew his body could take only so much of her nearness, and he didn't want to send the wrong message. Yet he knew how women could be. He didn't want her to read any more into the kiss than what was there.

A sudden desire to protect her, as well as himself, fell over him, and he quickly dropped his hand.

"Let me walk you to the door." He hurried around to the passenger side and helped her out of the car. They walked silently to her front door, each caught up in their own thoughts. This had been a strange evening, but Derek knew something special had transpired between them. She wasn't just his neighbor and client anymore. She was also his friend...and maybe more than that.

Macy pulled her keys from her handbag and met his gaze. "Thank you for letting me cry on your shoulder... and for bringing me home. Again, I'm sorry about missing our—"

"Don't." He stopped her with that one word. "You don't have to apologize about our meeting again. I should have known something must have come up for you not to show or call. I'm really sorry about Amber." He lifted his hand to touch her arm but stopped himself. "If you need anything—" he nodded toward his house "—you know where to find me."

They said good-night and Derek waited until she was in the house before he walked away. Things had definitely changed between them, and he wasn't sure how he felt about it.

Actually, he did know. She turned him on the way no other woman ever had. Knowing that, he knew he couldn't act on his attraction, but keeping his distance from her would probably be one of the toughest challenges he'd ever have to endure.

The next morning, Macy lay in bed thinking about the day before. She hadn't slept well and was glad she had the day off.

Hearing Jason playing outside, she thought about Derek. She didn't know why it was so important that he believed her when she told him she would never abandon her family, but it was. Her heart ached for him and Jason at what they must have gone through years ago. Yet she had the utmost respect for how Derek had stepped up to the plate to take care of his child. Jason was one of the happiest kids she had ever met, and she knew that had a lot to do with his home environment. It also said a lot about Derek. He didn't put his responsibilities on someone else but had changed his life around in order to be a stay-at-home dad. That said a lot about his character. That said a lot about him as a man.

She threw off the bedcovers and, wearing an over-size T-shirt and boy shorts, padded to the bathroom. She touched her lips. Thoughts of the kisses they had shared invaded her mind again as she looked at herself in the mirror. The day before had been such an emotional one, just thinking about it made her want to crawl back into bed and bury herself under the covers. But kissing Derek made her want to get to know him better. A lot better.

Chapter 8

Thursday. Macy didn't know if her Thursdays would ever be the same. Most days she found herself smiling easily at a memory of Noah, but on Thursday evenings, not so much. She missed him. For as many years as she could remember, she and Noah had eaten dinner together on Thursdays, unless one of them was out of town. If she had to pinpoint one thing she missed most about not having him around, it was their weekly dinners.

She moved around her large kitchen with all the familiarity of a person who cooked every day. With high-end stainless-steel appliances, granite countertops and enough food in the house to live on for a month, she loved cooking. But she hated cooking for just one, which was how the Thursday night dinner ritual had started. Since his wife's death years earlier, Noah had rarely eaten dinner at home. To ensure he'd get a home-cooked meal, Macy had insisted he have dinner with her at least one day a week.

She smiled at the thought. He had first complained about it being on Thursdays and not Sundays when normal folks had family dinners. He knew he was always welcome at her home, but she'd chosen Thursdays. It was the one day during the week they both had free.

Macy pulled the marinated steaks out of the refrigerator, along with the ingredients for a tossed salad. She had prepped the meat earlier that day, looking forward to grilling them that evening. Her mouth watered as she inhaled deeply the combined smell of soy sauce, lemon juice, garlic, parsley and other ingredients that made up her special sauce. Pulling a glass bowl from the cabinet and setting it on the granite countertop, she stopped in her tracks. Her emotions were suddenly getting the best of her.

"I'm not going to cry," she said to herself with conviction. Noah had told her that he didn't want her to shed any tears once he was gone.

He's in a better place. He's with Lorraine.

That thought made Macy smile. His wife, Lorraine, had been the love of his life. When she had passed away years earlier, remarrying had never crossed his mind. He had once told Macy he was a one-woman man and he had already had the woman he wanted. Their relationship was everything Macy wanted with her future husband. Assuming she'd one day have one.

"Stop." She placed her hands, palms down on the

counter. She wasn't about to go down that road tonight. Instead, she was going to have a nice dinner, some wine, and a relaxing evening.

Seeing all the food out on the counter, it looked as if she was making a meal for four or five people instead of just one.

"I don't want to eat alone," she murmured, tapping the tips of her nails against the countertop. She went in search of her cell phone to call the first person who came to mind. She just hoped he'd come. She couldn't handle hearing no tonight.

"Hello?" The deep baritone sound of his voice caressed her body like a silk dress. Man, she had it bad. Ever since that kiss in his office, then the one in his car a couple of weeks ago, she couldn't stop thinking about him.

"Hi, Derek. It's Macy."

"Hey, what's up?" Gone were the days when she would call him and it seemed as if he didn't want to be bothered with her. After all the time they were spending working on the plans for the medical complex, she now actually considered him a friend.

"Hello? Macy?"

"I'm sorry. I...um, was wondering if you could come over."

Silence filled the phone line. Macy's heart sank. She closed her eyes and pinched the bridge of her nose, bracing herself for a no.

"Are you okay?" he asked, worry in his voice. Macy wasn't sure what he had heard in her request, but she had tried to put as much cheer in her voice as she could.

"Yes, I'm fine. I guess I just need some company. For the past four or five years, whenever Noah and I were both in town, we had a standing Thursday-night dinner date. And…"

"I'll be right there." Derek disconnected without saying anything else.

Macy set the phone on the table near the sofa in the family room, surprised he had said yes. She took a quick glance around to ensure the house was presentable but quickly realized she wasn't dressed for company.

"Oh, crap." She headed for the stairs that would take her to the master bedroom with every intention of shedding her fitted T-shirt and yoga pants. Her usual attire after a long workday.

She made it to the third step when the doorbell rang. With a frustrated groan, she turned on her heels and headed to the door. A glance in the foyer's mirror showed her ponytail in place, with a few strands of hair framing her face. She hadn't touched up her makeup since that morning, but her appearance was going to have to do.

Macy swung the front door open and her breath hitched. She had only seen Derek in a T-shirt and jeans one other time, and today he looked just as sexy. The light blue T-shirt stretched across his solid chest and toned biceps. Her gaze traveled lower to his jeans that were a little faded on the front of the thigh, but dark everywhere else, and hung low on his hips. It looked as if he might have just stuck his feet into the first pair of

Air Jordans he could find, because his pant legs were partially in the high-tops and his shoes weren't tied.

Her gaze worked its way back up to his eyes, and it looked as if she wasn't the only one giving a once-over.

"Thank you for coming."

"No problem." He stepped over the threshold when she opened the door wider. "It worked out good since Jason clunked out early tonight and Keith's there."

"I'm sorry to just up and call, but…well, I'm glad you're here."

Derek followed her back to the kitchen and her cheeks heated, sensing he was checking her backside out.

"Can I get you something to drink? Beer? Water? Juice?" She stopped at the refrigerator, her hand on the handle before she turned back to him. She didn't see him smile much, but when he did, it made him look even more handsome.

"How about a beer?"

They worked together to prepare the meal, and Macy was glad she had taken a chance and called him.

"Steaks should be done in about five minutes," Derek said when he walked back into the kitchen, closing the sliding glass door behind him. "Are the vegetable skewers ready to be put on the grill?"

"Almost." Macy added pineapple and bell peppers to the last of the four skewers.

Derek leaned his hip against the counter, his arms folded across his chest. Macy wondered how he kept his body so tight, considering the number of hours he worked. She couldn't stop her gaze from traveling to his biceps, wondering how they would feel if she wrapped her hands around them. Or how it would feel to run her hands down his flat abs.

Stop. Stop. Stop, she silently chastised herself. There would be no touching, and she really shouldn't be looking. He had made it clear that he wasn't interested in anything serious.

The weekend after she and Derek had lunch, Macy had invited him and Jason to the Georgia Aquarium. Neither had been before, and she thought it would be a great opportunity for Tania to meet Jason. Of course, her niece had immediately fallen in love with Derek's son. And after spending hours with Derek, Macy knew she could easily fall for his charm. But she couldn't allow that to happen. She *was* searching and waiting for her happily-ever-after. Derek wasn't. They would never be able to have more than a friendship.

"When you and Noah used to have dinner together, did you always do the cooking?" Derek asked, interrupting her thoughts.

Macy nodded and arranged the skewers on a platter. "Most of the time. We went out sometimes, but since I love cooking…" Macy shrugged and slid the platter over to him. Their hands met and that electric charge she felt whenever they touched shot through her body.

She pulled her hands away and slid them down the sides of her thighs. "I appreciate you coming over. I just didn't feel like eating alone again."

He picked up the platter from the counter. "You can stop thanking me. I'd be a fool to pass up dinner with a beautiful woman."

Macy's mouth dropped open as she watched him leave the kitchen and head back out to the deck. As a man of few words, he had definitely shared a mouthful.

He thinks I'm beautiful. She grinned and rinsed off the tomatoes for the salad. She couldn't remember the last time someone had actually called her that, but the happiness suddenly swirling around inside of her reminded her of how good it felt to get a compliment from a nice-looking man.

Derek released a groan when he stepped out onto Macy's deck. Any man with a pulse would notice how gorgeous she was, but he hadn't planned to actually voice the sentiment. And by the way her eyes grew big and round, she was just as surprised to hear the words. He hoped she didn't make too much of his slip of the tongue. Just because he thought she was easy on the eyes didn't mean he had any intention of letting his attraction to her go anywhere.

He removed everything from the grill just as Macy stepped outside with plates and glasses.

"I was thinking that maybe we can eat out here." She set the items in the center of the octagon-shaped table. "Or do you think it's too hot?"

"It's definitely warm out here," he said, thinking that the weather wasn't the only thing heating his body, "but I think we could make it work."

"Great. We can always bring that large fan that's in the sunroom out here."

"Good idea. I'll grab it."

"Okay, and I'll bring the rest of the food out."

Derek stepped back into the house and made a left toward the sunroom off the family room. Why Macy needed such a large home was a mystery to him. At a glance, it appeared to be close to the same square footage as his, but he didn't have a sunroom.

They spent the next hour chatting and eating. Derek wasn't much of a talker, but Macy's personality seemed to draw him out, making him want to talk to her. They had witnessed the beginning of a sunset over the rooftops of some of the neighbors' homes. The sun's orange-red glow scattered across the sky and then slowly slipped behind the horizon.

His gaze took in Macy's profile, and the familiar stirring he felt whenever they were together was soon getting the best of him. He had to get a grip. And quickly. She was off-limits.

The next weekend, Macy lounged around the house with her sisters. It seemed Janna's schedule allowed her more time to visit them in Atlanta lately. As a supermodel, her days were usually filled with photo shoots around the world. She had flown in from LA the day before and was headed to Paris the next day. Macy treasured their times together.

Iris waddled into the room carrying a glass of juice. Six months pregnant, and Macy hadn't ever seen her look more beautiful. Married over a year to Nash Dupree, who was once known as the most eligible bachelor in Atlanta, Iris was literally glowing. But why shouldn't she be? She had an attentive husband who thought the sun only shined because of her and an adopted daughter, Tania, who worshiped the ground she walked on.

Macy couldn't believe it had already been a year since Nash and his biological niece, Tania, had come into their lives. When Tania got into trouble with the law, Nash hired Iris, a defense attorney, to keep her out of jail. Things didn't go as planned in court. Iris ended up being somewhat of a foster parent to Tania, which, in turn, brought her and Nash together. It had been a stressful time for all of them, but a wonderful union had come out of a bad situation, and now Macy not only had a niece, but two nephews on the way.

"It's good to see you taking some much-needed time off," Iris said, cutting into Macy's thoughts. She sat in the cushioned chair next to the sofa where Macy lounged.

"Yeah, actually, it feels pretty good. I'm so thankful to have Rachel on board. My life is still busier than I'd like, but having some assistance at the clinic really helps."

"Are you still volunteering at the shelter?"

Macy nodded. She spent two days a week at Three Meals, a day shelter that provided food, showers, clothing and computers to the homeless. The organization and the services they offered were close to her heart, especially since many people were only a paycheck away from homelessness.

"Okay, enough of the small talk," Janna said from the kitchen where she was loading the dishwasher with the lunch dishes. "How's it going with that hot neighbor of yours with the cute kid? Or should I say, how's it going with your soul mate?"

Macy lifted her head slightly from the pillow to glare at her sister. "He's not my soul mate." She dropped her head back on the pillow. "He's just the current man in my life who is sometimes bossy, irritating, and the only man I know who is never late for anything." Macy had never met a person who made such an issue about time. "These days he's not driving me as nutty as he used to."

"And?"

Macy hesitated. "And he makes my heart beat double time just thinking about him."

"I knew it!" Janna pounded on the counter. "You have never talked about a man as much as you talk about him. Not even when you almost married that loser fiancé of yours. The neighbor guy, uh, Derek, I bet he's your Mr. Right."

He was marriage material: great with kids, a cook, and he was the CEO of a multimillion-dollar company. Oh yeah, he was definitely marriage material. Lot of good that would do, though. Derek acted as if he'd rather give up a kidney before risking marriage again. No way was Macy going to allow herself to fall for someone who wasn't looking for forever the way she was.

When neither Iris nor Janna said anything, Macy turned to look at them, not surprised by the stupid grins on their faces.

"Macy has a boyfriend. Macy has a boyfriend," Janna said in a singsong voice.

"Would you quit it and grow up? I don't have a boy-friend. I just…"

"You just like him. A lot. I can't believe you're ac-tually admitting to liking someone."

Macy wasn't about to admit to her sisters that her feelings for Derek had gone way beyond "like" but were bordering on… Actually, she wasn't ready to admit what she was feeling these days. All she knew was that thoughts of him were still keeping her awake at night.

"So what's the problem? You like him, and the way Tania said he was looking at you that day at the aquar-ium, I have no doubt that he likes you, too," Iris said. "You say you want to get married. So maybe—"

"I am ready to get married, but I don't want to marry someone just to be marrying them. I want to be madly and passionately in love with a man." Macy twirled a lock of her hair around her finger. "I want the type of love that makes you warm all over just thinking about him. Or the type of love that makes your heart skip a beat when he walks into a room. And with that love, I want a dose of passion tossed in that makes my toes curl when his lips touch mine." Her mind took her back to the two kisses she and Derek had shared weeks ago. "I guess you can say I want my relationship to have the type of passion you and Nash have," she said to Iris.

"Oh, so you want to have sex on every flat surface or against any available wall," Janna cracked.

Iris's mouth dropped open. "I can't believe you said that! You make us sound like some horny teenagers."

Janna lifted an eyebrow. "Well."

Macy put her feet on the floor and laughed. She didn't know what she would do without her sisters. They were her strength when she was going through a tough time and comic relief whenever she needed a laugh.

"Well, I'm pretty sure I'll never have that with Derek. He hasn't even asked me out, unless you count that impromptu lunch." Macy didn't have time to be fawning over a man. At her age, it was time she found someone to settle down with and start having some babies of her own.

Over the past three months, she had taken on twelve infants as patients. Seeing their chubby little faces and holding their tiny bodies just made her want a family of her own that much more.

"Well…maybe *you* can ask him out," Iris suggested.

"Bad idea." Janna plopped down on the sofa next to Macy. "Nothing gets a man off his butt and into action like another man." She turned to Macy. "Levi is still asking about you. I think you should go out with him. Say the word and I'll call him today."

Macy crossed her legs and folded her arms across her chest. Levi, a male model who was one of the most gorgeous men Macy had ever laid eyes on, had asked her out a couple of times. Maybe it was time to finally say yes. But how would she be able to go out with someone else when she was crazy about Derek?

Unfortunately, Derek's ex-wife had ruined him for anyone else, as far as Macy was concerned. She didn't want to be one of those women to get with a man and think she could change his mind about being in a serious relationship.

She dropped her arms and turned slightly, her gaze landing on Janna. "Set it up. I'm free Friday night."

Macy couldn't remember the last time she'd been on a date. She had gone dateless not from lack of suitors, but from her own lack of interest. Now she only wanted to date men she could see a future with, and that definitely wasn't Levi.

She glanced at him from the passenger seat of his sporty Jaguar. He was a nice enough guy, but she felt no connection. None. Her body didn't tingle when he hugged her. Hell, she didn't even go all fangirl like some women would have when she opened the door to him.

"Have you been here before?" Levi asked when they pulled up to the tapas bar in Brookhaven. Besides the R&B music playing through the speakers, they had ridden in silence for most of the drive.

"Actually, I haven't." She unfastened her seat belt. "I have heard some great things about it, though."

"Yeah, it's a cool place to hang out. And I'm glad you'll have a first with me." He winked and flashed his million-dollar smile before exiting the car. Macy watched him stroll around to the passenger side. It was no wonder he had been recruited into the modeling industry at fifteen. Over six feet tall, with a lean body and a handsome face that would make any woman take a second look, he was not only *hot*, but he was a perfect gentleman. Too bad he was so young. At twenty-nine, he was six years her junior and didn't look a day over twenty. At least Derek was only two years younger than her.

She gave herself a mental shake. Her whole reason for going out with Levi was to get her mind off Derek. Yet she thought about him every few minutes.

"Ready?"

Macy nodded and accepted his hand. She stepped out of the car and adjusted the low-cut blouse and short skirt Janna had insisted she wear on the date.

He led Macy into the restaurant and it began—the stares. Macy was used to being ignored in public when she was out with Janna, but with Levi, it felt different. She couldn't believe how women approached him as if she weren't even there.

They walked through the cozy restaurant, weaving through tables that were, in Macy's opinion, too close together. On the way to their seats, Levi gave at least ten autographs, and Macy was pretty sure a couple of women slipped their telephone numbers into his jacket pocket.

"Sorry about that." He pulled out Macy's chair and waited until she was seated. "Some days are crazier than others with my fans." He shrugged.

Somehow, Macy wasn't convinced that he was sorry. In fact, he looked as if he was trying to draw attention to their table.

"Is something wrong?" she asked. He stood next to his chair, making a show of taking off his jacket.

"No, just getting a little warm."

"Excuse me, aren't you Levi Stevens?" a young woman in her early twenties asked from the next table.

"Yes. I am."

The table of five giggled like schoolgirls and Macy rolled her eyes.

"This is going to be a long night," she mumbled, and opened her menu. This would be the last time she went out with anyone Janna suggested.

Chapter 9

Derek set his pencil down on the drafting table and rubbed his eyes. Frustration coursed through his veins and it was all Macy's fault. Something had changed between them. He wasn't sure when it happened, but she had somehow penetrated the invisible wall he had carefully built around his heart.

He stood suddenly. A low growl rumbled inside his chest and he paced around his home office. He couldn't stop thinking about her. He had already called her several times, using the excuse of having questions regarding her project to get her to call him back. This was crazy. She was his neighbor and his client. Nothing else. Yet here he was on a Friday night, with the house to himself since Keith had taken Jason out, and all Derek could think about was her.

He stopped and shoved his hands into his pants pockets, his gaze aimed heavenward. What the heck was he going to do? He couldn't make a play for her, knowing what he knew. She wanted marriage and kids. He didn't. On the other hand, it was getting harder and harder to keep his hands and lips to himself. Everything about the woman turned him on, from her sweet smile and her curvaceous body to her brilliant mind. Except for her tendency toward being late all the time, she was the perfect package.

"No!" He shook his head. He wasn't looking for, nor did he need, the perfect package. He had to remember that before he did something stupid. He blew out a breath. "Fresh air. I need some fresh air. But first…"

He grabbed his phone from the corner of the drafting table and called Macy's cell. Again, her voice mail picked up.

"Hey, Macy, this is Derek. Give me a call when you get a chance. It doesn't matter the time. I want to run a few possible changes to the medical complex design by you."

Why was he torturing himself? Unable to stop the unrest floating through his body, he shoved his cell phone into his pocket and walked outside to the front stoop. He glanced at Macy's dark house. "Where are you?" Running his hand over his low haircut, he was convinced—he had it bad.

Clearly, I have lost my frickin' mind. Never had he obsessed over a woman.

He leaned against one of the thick columns that framed the porch-like stoop of his house and gazed out into the night, the quietness almost deafening. He had been in Atlanta for three months now. For the most part, he was settled in and had established a good routine, juggling work and getting Jason to and from school with the help of Keith, Macy and another baby-sitter that Macy had helped him find.

The only thing he still hadn't worked out was his feelings for Macy. Actually, that hadn't been a problem until recently. Before, he'd had his feelings in check. Yet his mind and heart weren't working together in this situation.

Headlights from a vehicle turned onto the street and the car pulled into Macy's circular driveway. Sure that it wasn't hers, Derek leaned forward to get a better look.

A tall man—or should he say, *kid*—exited the driver's side and jogged around to the passenger side of the car. When he opened the door, Macy stepped out and Derek sucked in a breath.

"Damn, she looks good."

He had seen her dressed up on a couple of occasions, but tonight she looked downright sexy in an almost sheer, long-sleeved blouse and a too-short black skirt. With the fall weather being unseasonably warm, she was still able to wear sandals. And not just any sandals. Even from where he stood, he could see they were at least four inches tall with a strap around the ankle and jewels across the top of her foot.

Damn, she looks good, he thought again. *But who the hell is this guy with his arm around her waist?* Derek's hands balled into fists at his sides when Macy placed her hand on the man's arm and smiled up at him. *If she kisses him, so help me...* Instead, her date placed a lingering kiss against her cheek and strolled back to his car.

Macy waited by her front door until her date left. When she turned and walked toward Derek's house, he stood straighter. Had she seen him?

She carefully maneuvered through the grass in her high heels. Her normally sexy strut was hindered. "Crap," he heard her grumble when her heel sank into the soil.

Derek stepped out of the shadows just as she crossed the invisible property line, giving him a better view. Desire traveled through his body as she moved closer, and he got a better look at her appearance. Her hair, curled at the ends, covered part of her face as she monitored each step she took. Normally, she sported a ponytail, but he loved seeing her hair hanging loose around her shoulders. The sheer blouse covered a camisole, and that damn skirt that had him salivating earlier was shorter than he'd originally thought.

His traitorous body reacted immediately when his gaze finally landed on her toned thighs and killer legs.

"What the hell were you doing with that guy?" The words flew out of his mouth before he could stop them.

Macy stopped short. "Excuse me?"

"You heard me."

She gripped her clutch purse tighter. "Are you drunk?" She studied him with concern.

"No. I'm not drunk." He rubbed a hand across his forehead and released a noisy breath. He stood only inches away, his hands itching to touch her. "How are you just going to go on a date? What about *us*?"

"What?" She narrowed her eyes and stared at him as if he had lost his mind. "There is no *us*. Besides, the last time I checked, I was a grown woman who could go out with whomever I want." She huffed, pushing hair away from her face. "You know what? Coming over here was a bad idea. I'm going home." She turned to leave.

"Don't." He reached for her hand and she stopped. He knew he wasn't thinking straight, but at the moment he didn't care. He was tired of denying his feelings for her, and it was time he did something about them.

Macy studied him. Besides looking a little tired, he seemed fine. What could explain his behavior? Why would he care if she had gone on a date, and what the heck was he talking about when he had asked, "What about us?"

He had called her several times during the night, and at one point in the evening, she had thought about returning his call. Especially when she deduced that Levi was an attention hound. He loved being in the spotlight. With the number of girls and women out tonight who recognized him from commercials and covers of popular magazines, Levi was in his element.

After dinner, she had insisted on him taking her home. It had been nice to get out, but there wouldn't be a second date. Besides, most of her evening was spent thinking about Derek. When she spotted him out front as Levi turned into her driveway, she had decided then she'd stop by his house. Now she wasn't so sure if that had been a good idea.

"I'm not crazy," Derek said, as if reading her mind. "I just…"

He pulled her to his body and she swallowed hard at their closeness. His familiar scent washed over her like a loving caress, her self-control weakening. She might have thought about him all evening, but her thoughts hadn't taken this route. Never had he regarded her with such desire swimming in his eyes. His gaze held hers but quickly moved to her lips. It was as if he was contemplating his next move. He lowered his mouth closer to hers, but then he pulled back slightly. She wanted to scream, *Kiss me already*, but instead she waited.

His large hands cupped the sides of her face and he mumbled something she couldn't understand. Before she could speak, he captured her lips in a searing kiss. Her thoughts jumbled inside her head. She didn't know what had gotten into him, but whatever it was, she was all in. He kissed her with an eagerness that left no doubt they wanted the same thing. At the moment, she didn't care that he wasn't looking for anything long-term. All she knew was that she needed him, desired him right then and there.

She whimpered when his lips left hers, and he placed a trail of kisses down her cheek and on down to her neck. When he made his way back up to her mouth, he placed a feathery kiss against her lips.

"Come on." His low growl caught her off guard. Was he angry with her? He grabbed her by the hand and pulled her into his house, slamming the door once they were inside. Before she could mumble a word, he backed her up against the wall. "Do you know what you do to me?" he asked, his voice filled with emotion. She sensed he battled with staying in control and he was losing. Unfortunately, she couldn't help him. She had never wanted a man the way she wanted him in all of her life.

Her body shivered under his perusal. She wasn't afraid of him, but his unfamiliar behavior ignited excitement and caution at the same time.

"I want you," he muttered, his fingers making quick work of unbuttoning her blouse. He slipped it down her shoulders and then quickly relieved her of the satin camisole. His gaze zoned in on the strapless bra that barely contained her full breasts. Oh yeah. They wanted the same thing. He glided his large hand slowly down the side of her neck, his fingertips cool against the heated skin of her chest. If he was trying to torture her with his touch, it was working.

"Derek," she said breathlessly, unable to form any other word as lust flowed through her veins and picked up speed. He had barely touched her. Yet the throbbing between her thighs and the pounding in her chest had her barely holding on.

Was this what passion felt like? To want a man so badly she was willing to forgo all common sense? Her body had betrayed her a number of times before when he was near, but tonight, the heat that was bouncing around to every nerve ending was sparking a desire within her that needed to be satisfied.

She wasn't sure who moved first, but their mouths

met somewhere in the middle, and he kissed her with a hunger that rivaled any kiss she had ever experienced. Her arms went around his neck of their own accord. She had dreamed about this moment more than once, never thinking she would ever be this close to him again. It had been weeks since his lips had touched hers, and boy, had she missed them.

Memories of the kiss they'd shared in his office invaded her mind. As it had then, his skilled tongue darted in and out, thoroughly exploring the inner recesses of her mouth.

A moan tumbled from Macy and she tightened the hold she had around his neck. His hard body ground against hers and it was taking everything she had to hold on and not puddle to the floor.

"Derek," she said on a shaky breath when he lifted his head. "I… I." She couldn't get her thoughts, let alone her words, together as his hands moved over her breasts and squeezed. Her eyes drifted closed.

"I need you," he said roughly. He pulled down the side zipper of her skirt and let it slide over her hips and onto the floor around her ankles. "I need you now." Bending slightly, he gripped the back of her thighs, and he surprised her by hoisting her into his arms. He headed for the stairs.

Macy tightened her legs around his waist, impressed by his strength as he carried her up the semi-spiral staircase, nipping at her covered breasts with his teeth. Somehow, he managed to unhook her strapless bra without missing a step, and dropped the lacy material to the floor. His behavior was so unlike that of the straitlaced man she had first met months ago.

The smell of vanilla floated to Macy's nose. The bedroom, lit only by a stream of moonlight shining through the small windows near the ceiling, was similar in size to hers, but the bed was humongous.

Derek's mouth was on one breast the moment he laid her on the bed and climbed up next to her. As his tongue swirled around her taut nipple, he slid her panties down her legs. She wiggled and kicked them the rest of the way off, suddenly realizing she was still in her sandals. She started to speak, but Derek went to her other nipple and bit down gently, sending a tingle to the soles of her feet. Suddenly the shoes didn't matter.

"Derek." Her hoarse whisper sounded foreign to her own ears, the pleading in her voice clear. "I can't wait." She had never been so bold as to tell a man she wanted him, but tonight she needed him to know.

He lifted his head slightly and traced his fingertip across her lower lip. "I have dreamed about this moment more times than I can remember."

"Me, too," she whispered and tugged on his shirt. "Only problem—you have on way too many clothes."

His lips twitched before turning up into a full-blown grin. "I guess I do."

He stood and quickly slipped out of his clothes. Placing a couple of foil packages on the bedside table, he climbed back onto the bed. Instead of picking up where he left off, he lay on his side and perused her naked body. His hand seared a path from her neck, down between her breasts, stopping just before he reached the juncture between her thighs.

"You're absolutely breathtaking."

What she saw in his eyes made her insides quiver. His gaze held the same look that she'd seen in his eyes earlier. Desire. Need. Longing.

She turned and raked her fingers through the wisp of hair on his chest, before circling one of his nipples. He had awakened a fervor within her that she had every intention of exploring. Nudging him onto his back, she lowered her head, snaked her tongue out and twirled it around his nipple.

Derek cursed under his breath, his fingers deep in her hair. His tormented groan made her want to explore more. She knew a man's nipples were just as sensitive as a woman's and wanted to give him the same pleasure he'd given her. When she captured his other nipple between her teeth, she almost smiled at his string of curses, surprised by his potty mouth. Oh yeah, this was going to be fun.

She slid her hand slowly down his body until she reached his rigid shaft. Now she was the one moaning. He felt so good, thick and long. She tightened her hand around his length and he sucked in a breath, his hands fisting the bedsheets as he bucked against her touch.

"Macy," he growled.

Stroking. Squeezing. She picked up speed and he grew within her grasp. The more she touched him, the more moisture built between her own thighs, turning her on even more.

"You like that?" she asked boldly.

"I love it," he said between gritted teeth. "But, baby—" he jerked and covered her hand with his, slowing her moves "—if you keep doing that…"

With quickness, he slipped out of her grasp and had her flat on her back before she could react. "I think you like torturing me." He ran his fingers through her hair and covered her mouth with the same thirst as earlier, sliding his tongue easily between her parted lips.

A passionate fluttering bubbled in her stomach and her sex throbbed with need. *This is what passion feels like*. This is what she'd been longing for, what she needed. What she needed now.

She wiggled beneath him and snatched her mouth from his. "Derek," she panted, her eagerness sprouting to explosive proportions. "I can't wait. I need you."

His gaze studied her face. "I need you, too, baby," he finally said and sheathed himself.

They were really going to do this. How many times had she imagined this moment? Thought about what it would feel like to have his mouth on hers, his hands caressing her body and their bodies joined together?

Derek nudged her legs apart. His erection pressed against her inner thigh, sending a whole new wave of desire pumping through her veins. One hand slid down her side to the swell of her hip, his other braced on the pillow near her head. Without breaking eye contact, he entered her. *Oh my…* Her sex tightened around his length and she sucked in a breath. At first his moves were slow, but he quickly picked up speed. It was as if angels were singing in the background as heat soared through her body. They rocked together in perfect sync.

Oh yes. Oh yes. The chant inside her mind matched his thrusts and Macy gripped his thick biceps, fighting for control.

"De-rek," she panted, her hands sliding against his sweat-covered skin. A hot tide of liquid heat suddenly consumed her. She couldn't hold on. "Derek!" she screamed, her body bucking wildly when an orgasm gripped her like an electric shock. Stars flitted behind her closed lids and her breath came in short spurts. She tried to catch her breath. In and out. He didn't stop.

Not giving her time to recover, Derek increased his pace and Macy knew he wasn't far behind. Within seconds, his body jerked uncontrollably. A guttural growl tore through the quietness of the room as his release came hard and fierce.

Out of breath, he dropped his head to the space between her head and shoulder but lifted it slightly in order not to crush her. Macy held him tight, her chest heaving up and down as if she had just finished a marathon. A deep feeling of satisfaction settled within her and she closed her eyes. He had taken her to a level of passion she'd never known existed, and she would never be the same.

"That. Was. Frickin'. Amazing," Derek said, lying next to her, still breathing hard.

"I agree," she finally said after a long silence. "I agree."

A short while later, after a trip to the bathroom, they lay sated. Derek wrapped his arm around Macy's waist and he pulled her close, her back to his chest. He released a satisfied sigh, the tension from earlier a distant memory. Nuzzling her neck, she wiggled under his touch.

"That tickles." She giggled like a schoolgirl. Derek couldn't believe what they had just shared. Had someone told him months ago that he would be crazy about this woman to the point of almost taking her right there on his staircase, he would have told them they were insane. He hadn't had any expectations because he had never planned to have her in this way. But now that he'd had a taste of her, he couldn't imagine himself with anyone else. They would never be able to go back to the way things were.

"If you keep moving like that," he whispered into her hair, "you're going to get something started again. I'm trying to be good and let you take a break before we go for round two."

"I'm ready. You're the one who's still gasping for air."

Derek chuckled. "Oh, so now you're trying to talk all big. Just a moment ago, I had you screaming my name."

Macy laughed. She didn't deny it.

His hand roamed the length of her body, taking in every dip and curve. He cupped her breasts and their moans filled the air. "Aw, baby." Her butt rotated against his length and he moved with her, gripping her tighter. If he wasn't careful, he was going to come right then and there. His body vibrated with need and he had to have her again.

As if reading his mind, Macy pulled away from him and grabbed the other condom from the bedside table.

A grin spread across his mouth when she ripped the packet open with her teeth. She didn't come across as the type of woman who would take the lead, but he could honestly say he liked this side of her.

He gasped when her soft hand covered his length. Stroking him, she ran her thumb across his tip and he grounded his teeth. He watched her with lowered lids and tried to hang on as she sheathed him. She definitely knew what she was doing. Her slow, torturous moves were going to be the death of him.

"This time—" she lowered her face, only inches from his "—I'm on top."

An hour later, Derek lay on his back, dozing off and on with Macy in his arms. He rubbed his eyes and stared up at one of the two skylights above his bed, seeing the stars that sparkled in the night.

When he lived in Cincinnati, he hadn't been as sexually active as he'd been before and during marriage, but he had had a couple of friends with benefits—to knock off the edge occasionally. But sex with Macy was different. Amazing. Exhilarating. Fantastic. Two rounds of lovemaking and it was safe to say she could easily become an addiction. He wanted her again. He was known for always being in control, so tonight his behavior was way out of character. Stripping her down in his foyer and barely getting her to his bedroom before having his way with her was so not like him.

Macy released a soft moan. The sensual sound flowed through him like hot lava, making him hard all over again. He couldn't ever remember having a hunger for a woman the way he had for Macy. Twice with her wasn't enough.

His house alarm chirped.

Oh, shit.

Macy's head jerked up at the same time as his. Despite the limited amount of moonlight shining through, he could see her sleepy gaze darting around the room.

Jason. All Derek could think about was his son tearing through the house looking for him. And then Derek remembered Macy's clothes. Keith was definitely going to harass him about the items strewn through the house, leaving a trail up the stairs.

Derek placed a kiss on the side of Macy's head and peeled his arm from around her.

"Stay put. I'll be right back."

He leaped up and hurried across the room to his dresser, snatching the first pair of gym shorts his hand touched. His heart pounded loudly inside his chest as he pulled a T-shirt over his head. The last thing he needed was for Jason to storm into the bedroom and start asking questions about Ms. Macy being in the bed.

Rushing out into the hallway, Derek ran into Keith, who had just made it to the top of the landing, Jason asleep in his arms.

His brother shook his head and grinned. "Damn, man. When you jump back on the horse, you go all out, huh?" He nodded toward Macy's pink, lacy bra sitting at the top of the stairs.

Derek snatched up the garment and balled it into his hand. He didn't know what to say. Hell, what could he say? *I just had the most amazing sex of my adult life?*

Nah, Keith would rag him till no end. Chances were, Derek was going to be hearing about this night for many years to come.

"I see you guys finally made it back." Derek reached for Jason, but Keith turned him away.

"What?" Derek said through gritted teeth. "If you have something to say, just say it."

Keith stared at him for a moment before speaking, the stupid grin still on his face. "I'm glad you finally took care of your needs, but you might want to be a little more discreet in the future." He nodded his head toward a sleeping Jason. "What if he was awake? You know he would be asking fifty million questions and would be breaking his neck to get back there to Macy." He paused. "I assume that piece of lace you're holding belongs to her."

"Yeah, she's in the room." Derek held the garment tighter. "And you're right. This is not the appropriate behavior for me to be having with a four-year-old in the house. It won't be happening again."

Keith nodded and proceeded to Jason's room. Derek knew his brother was right. There was no way anyone, least of all his son, should've witnessed his indiscretion. But tonight he hadn't been thinking about anything or anybody but Macy.

He bounded down the stairs and grabbed her clothes before heading back to the bedroom. When he walked in, Macy was sitting on the edge of the bad, the sheet wrapped around her.

"So it won't be happening again, huh?" Macy spat out. *Oh, damn.*

"Baby, you misunderstood what I meant." She let the sheet drop and snatched her clothes from his hands. When he'd said it wouldn't happen again, he meant that he would be more discreet. Yet, now that he was thinking with a clear mind, he reminded himself that he wasn't looking for anything serious. Then again, seeing the disappointment in Macy's eyes, he knew he had to make things right.

She slipped on her bra and camisole, refusing to look at him. "I can't believe I let this happen," she mumbled as she haphazardly adjusted her skirt and stepped into her stilettos.

When Derek reached out to touch her arm, she shook him off. He blocked her path when she headed for the door.

"It's not what you thought. I only meant we'll have to use more discretion next time."

"There won't be a next time," she said, as if she didn't believe his explanation.

"Macy, come on. Granted, I hadn't planned for any of this to happen, but I'm not sorry it did. We both wanted this."

"I'm not so sure about that right now, Derek. I'll call you tomorrow about the project." She skirted around him and rushed from the room.

"Just wait." He stuffed his feet into a pair of Nikes he had near the front door. "You shouldn't leave like this," he said to her retreating back. "Macy." She kept walking and seemed to pick up speed as she strode across his yard and then hers. "Macy!"

She stopped when she arrived at her door but didn't

turn to look at him. "What's there to talk about, Derek? You've made it clear that you're not looking for anything serious and that what just happened shouldn't have happened." She unlocked her door and walked in with him right on her heels.

Derek might not have meant for it to happen the way it had, but now that they had shared something special, he wasn't ready to just walk away.

"Go away with me this weekend," he blurted out. Macy appeared as shocked by his words as he was that they had slipped out of his mouth. It was too late to retract them, and Derek could honestly admit that he didn't want to. "Come to Miami with me."

Chapter 10

"What?" Macy finally found her voice. Derek was sending so many mixed signals she didn't know what to think.

"I'm leaving for Miami Sunday morning for a meeting. We have a huge project starting there soon and I need to go over some logistics before we start." He leaned against her kitchen counter and faced her. "I'm taking the company's jet and there is more than enough room for you. Come with me. We'll do a little sightseeing Sunday after we land, and then we can have a nice romantic dinner Sunday night. And before you say you have to work, I already know you're off Monday and Tuesday."

Macy didn't know what to say about the unexpected offer. She wanted to say yes, but she wasn't looking for an affair. She was ready to settle down. Settling for a sexual partner, even with someone like Derek, wasn't enough.

"I can't."

He approached her and wrapped his strong arms around her waist, the scent of his cologne making her weak in the knees.

"Why not?" His voice had dropped an octave and desire glistened in his intense brown eyes. The man was wreaking havoc on her body and probably had no idea just how he affected her.

"I want more than an affair, Derek." Her hands rested on his solid chest as she fingered the collar of the T-shirt he had hastily slipped into. "I *deserve* more than just an affair."

He dropped his forehead to hers and blew out a frustrated breath. "I know you do, baby, but right now—" he lifted his head "—this is all I can give you."

She pulled out of his arms. "Then whatever this is between us can't happen. I like you…a lot, but I'm thirty-five years old, Derek. My days of dating someone whose personal goals don't line up with mine are done. I want the husband and the two-point-five kids."

Derek ran his hand over his head. "I know—" he met her gaze "—and you're right. You do deserve more than an affair. Unfortunately, I'm not looking for anything serious in my life right now. I've been there and done that. As you know, things with my ex ended very badly. I don't know if I'm willing to go through something like that again."

"I can't guarantee we'll fall madly in love and live

happily ever after." Macy stood before him, struggling not to give in to his request. "What I can guarantee you, though, is that I would never hurt you, nor would I ever leave you and Jason the way your ex-wife did."

She started to walk away from him, but he stopped her with a hand on her arm.

"I care about you and I know you're not my ex. Hell, you're nothing like her. There is definitely something special between us and I want to explore what that is. But…"

She cupped his cheek with her hand and stared into his eyes. "I know. I care about you, too, and I understand." She placed a soft kiss against his lips and went to the front door.

Derek reluctantly followed her. When he stepped outside, he placed his hand on the door, stopping her from closing it. "I can't promise you forever…right now, but I would like us to explore whatever this is between us."

She held his gaze, debating whether or not she could handle dating him without knowing for sure if he would ever want the same things she wanted. Her gaze dropped to his lips. The same lips that had given her so much pleasure only hours ago.

"Okay, but I'm still not going to Miami with you." She tried to keep a straight face but failed. A broad grin spread across her mouth. "But I will let you take me out to dinner when you return."

He smiled back at her. "Then dinner it is. Take care and I'll talk to you in a few days."

Macy closed the door behind him and leaned against

it. What a night of firsts. It had started with her date
with Levi, which turned out to be a waste of time. But
then she somehow ended up tangled in the bedsheets
with Derek. *A heck of a night.*

She pushed away from the door, turned off the
kitchen light and went upstairs to her bedroom. Her
time with Derek tonight would be forever engrained
in her mind. Her body still tingled from the way he'd
kissed her, touched her and took his time making love
to her. A shiver shot through her at the memory of how
good they were together. She had dreamed of being
with Derek intimately, but her fantasies were no match
for reality. He made love to her body the way he did
everything else—with precision.

When Macy reached the top landing, she turned off
the stairwell light and glanced toward the large window
that allowed moonlight to spill into the hallway. She
couldn't believe how fast she had fallen for Derek. A
part of her knew she should pull back and take heed to
the fact that he wasn't looking for anything long-term.
Yet that little glimmer of hope traipsing through her
body made her want to see how things between them
turned out. She just hoped she didn't end up with a
broken heart.

Derek pulled into the parking lot of Macy's clinic.
They had an appointment to meet with the builder at
the new location, and Derek had offered to pick Macy
up and take her to lunch first. He wanted to spend time
with her. He couldn't explain it. In the past three years,
he had gone out with a few women casually, but never

more than twice. Yet Macy had not only garnered more than a few dates out of him, but had somehow gotten under his skin.

The past few weeks of dating her had been the most fun he'd had in a very long time. From their Thursday date nights to their afternoon trysts at her place, Derek couldn't get enough of her. His life was definitely changing for the better. In his wildest dreams, he never could have imagined suddenly becoming a millionaire, moving to Atlanta and then falling for a cutie-pie pediatrician who was always late for everything.

Derek climbed out of his Mercedes and headed to the front entrance of Macy's clinic. Her taking on another doctor months ago seemed to be a good move. Her business had increased thirty percent in the past year and for a while, she had been the only doctor on staff. It wasn't until her sister Iris insisted she needed more help that she brought Rachel aboard, giving her more flexibility.

Derek stepped into the colorful reception area. Four children played in the area to his right. A couple of parents sat nearby, talking to each other. Derek approached the receptionist.

"Hey, Derek. It's good to see you again." The twenty-something-year-old woman with a short Afro and big hoop earrings smiled up at him.

"Hey, Cindy. Do you know if your boss is ready?"

"I'm not sure, but I'll let her know you're here."

"Thanks."

Derek moved to the side and out of the way for a parent who had just walked in with a little boy about

Jason's age. He looked too heavy for her to be carrying, but he had to admit the kid didn't look well.

"Hi, I'm Vanessa Milton. I called earlier regarding my son running a fever."

"Oh yes, Mrs. Milton. Dr. Rachel will be able to see your son shortly."

"*Nooo*, I want Dr. Carter," the little boy who Derek thought was asleep whined. Derek was amazed that he would even have an opinion about whom he saw.

"I know, baby, but I told you, she's busy today." He started crying and Derek sympathized with the mother. Jason was at the age where he wanted what he wanted, and it often took Derek time to get his son to see reason. Times were definitely different from when he grew up. Whatever his mother or father said was law and there was no negotiating.

"Hey, what's going on out here?" Macy seemed to come out of nowhere, her handbag over her shoulder. Derek didn't think he would ever get used to the way his body thrummed whenever he saw her. And apparently he wasn't the only person Macy had an effect on. At the sound of her voice, the little boy immediately stopped crying and struggled to get out of his mother's arms.

"Hi, Dr. Carter," he mumbled.

"Hi, Jimmy, what're all the tears for?" She bent to the child's level and opened her arms to him. Over Jimmy's shoulder, Macy glanced up at Derek and smiled. He couldn't help smiling back.

She moved the child's blond hair from his forehead, feeling for a fever as she spoke soothing words to him.

It was no wonder the kid insisted on seeing her. She was amazing with him. The smile slipped from her face and was replaced by concern. She picked him up and he wrapped his arms around her neck, resting his head against her shoulder.

Derek could already tell she had no intention of leaving before checking the little guy out. *So much for lunch and being on time for our meeting.*

Her gaze met his and she sent him a sympathetic smile with a silent *I'm sorry.*

"I'll wait," he responded quietly and nodded toward some empty chairs. Her slight nod told him she'd heard him. Seeing the soothing effect she had on the little boy did something to Derek. Day after day, her actions, her compassion and the way she treated both him and Jason reminded him how different she was from his ex-wife.

Derek rubbed his hand over his chest as he took a seat in the far corner of the waiting room. The strong emotional pull he experienced with Macy was something he hadn't felt in a very long time, and it scared the hell out of him.

When Macy finished with Jimmy, she hurried to her office for her handbag. Derek had been waiting twenty-five minutes. Or at least she hoped he was still waiting. *So much for clearing her afternoon schedule.* She knew how he felt about being on time, and though their appointment with the contractor wasn't for another hour, she had been looking forward to lunch with Derek.

"You know I would have taken care of Jimmy, don't you?" Rachel leaned against the doorjamb with her arms folded across her chest, a knowing look on her face. "Or is it that you're just a sucker for a cute little boy with tears in his eyes?"

"He *is* cute, isn't he?" she said of Jimmy and grinned. She never could stand to see children cry.

"I saw your man sitting out there waiting for you. He must really care about you to hang out in a waiting room with children running around."

Macy smiled, knowing her friend was waiting for some details. They hadn't had a chance to really talk in the last couple of weeks due to their schedules.

"By the silly grin on your face, I'd say the feelings are mutual."

"He's very special to me."

Macy grabbed her handbag from the bottom drawer of her desk and pulled out her makeup compact. She couldn't believe that after several weeks, Derek still made her a little nervous…and horny. Seeing him standing in the waiting room earlier, looking as if he'd stepped off the cover of *GQ*, sent a sweet thrill pulsing through her body.

"But?"

Macy glanced over her shoulder at Rachel. "But what?"

"You said he was very special to you, but I have a feeling you wanted to say more. What's really going on between you and Derek?"

Macy shoved her makeup back into her bag before returning her attention to Rachel.

"I'm afraid I might get hurt."

Rachel's brows drew together. "Why? Why would you even think that?"

Without giving too much detail, Macy told her how Derek was divorced and wasn't looking to get married again or have any more children.

Rachel moved farther into the office and leaned on the corner of the desk. Macy knew what she was thinking. She had thought it herself at least a thousand times—she was playing with fire. After almost marrying a man who couldn't fully commit to her, Macy knew she should walk away from Derek and not look back. Yet...

"I think Derek is wonderful," Rachel said, interrupting Macy's thoughts.

"But."

"But Macy, you can't settle for less than you want. Everyone who knows you knows you want to get married and have a family. Don't settle. If he's been honest about not wanting anything serious, you have to get out before you lose your heart to him."

Macy wanted to curl up under her desk and hide. It was too late. She had already fallen for Derek. She loved everything about him, from that sexy grin he flashed every now and then to his brilliant mind. He was everything she ever wanted in a man.

"Oh no. It's too late, isn't it? You're in love with him."

Macy couldn't look at her friend. She thought she could handle dating Derek without any expectations, but clearly she was wrong.

"Macy, you—"

Macy lifted her hand. "I know. I screwed up." She

stood and grabbed her purse. She had left Derek waiting long enough.

"So what are you going to do?"

"I don't know. I can't walk away, but…" She let the words hang in the air. She refused to believe he would break her heart. Besides, she knew he cared for her, and right now, that would have to be enough.

Chapter 11

A week later, Macy rushed through the hallway, following the instructions she was given from the school's secretary to get to the nurse's office. Jason was sick, and since the school couldn't reach his father or Keith, they had called her. Derek had listed her as one of the emergency contacts on Jason's intake form.

How did single parents do it? How did they juggle work, a household and sick kids? She couldn't imagine handling that type of responsibility on her own.

"Hi, I'm Dr. Macy Carter, here to pick up Jason Lo—"

"Ms. Macy," came the small voice to the left of the nurse's desk. Jason walked toward her without his usual enthusiasm and Macy's heart tightened seeing the tears in his eyes.

"Ah, sweetheart." She bent down and he walked

into her arms, sniffling. "What's wrong?" She kissed the side of his forehead, noting he had a slight temperature, and rubbed his back. Without thinking, she lifted him into her arms, wanting to hold him. He was heavier than he looked, but by the grip his little arms had around her neck, it was safe to say he needed the hug she offered.

"My stomach is sick," he mumbled against her neck.

Smiling at his words and casting a quick glance at the nurse, she held him tighter. "Ah, we'll have to see if we can make it better."

She sat down with him, his legs straddling her lap as he snuggled more into her neck. She asked the nurse a few questions, wondering if they had given him anything and whether or not he had eaten. This was the first time that she had ever been in this position—picking up a sick child from school. She had to admit, it made her feel motherly. She hated that Jason was sick and knew scenarios like this were such a small part of motherhood. Yet she embraced the experience.

Macy stood with Jason, who was now asleep in her arms, and gathered her handbag and his backpack.

"Again, Dr. Carter, I'm sorry I had to bother you, but we couldn't reach Jason's dad or his uncle. You were the next person on the list."

"It's not a problem at all. I'm glad you called me." They spoke for a few minutes longer before Macy left the building. Thankfully, she had thought to grab one of the booster seats they had at the clinic.

Once Jason was settled in the backseat, she tried

Derek's cell phone again. When it went to voice mail, she called Louise.

"Good afternoon, Price Architecture. May I help you?" Louise's friendly voice floated over the telephone line.

"Hi, Louise, this is Macy. Is Derek available?"

"Well, hello there. It's always nice to hear from you," she greeted Macy. "I'm sorry, dear, but Derek has had several back-to-back meetings outside the office today. May I take a message for him?"

Macy told her about the school calling her and that she was taking Jason home with her.

"Oh no, they must have called while our phone systems were temporarily down. It wasn't for more than fifteen minutes."

"That's probably what happened."

"Well, I have Derek's schedule. If he's not picking up his phone, I can call the company that he's meeting with."

"That's all right, Louise. You don't have to go through all of that. My afternoon was a little light and my appointments reassigned. So don't bother him right now. When he gets a break, have him give me a call."

They said their goodbyes and Macy headed home. She glanced over her shoulder at Jason periodically to check on him, his soft snores filling the interior of the car. It was somewhat weird to have a little one riding with her. Tania was the only child that she had a personal relationship with outside of work, but Macy had missed the early years of Tania's life. Tania was sixteen when Iris and Nash got together.

Macy's stomach churned with anxiety. Her biological clock was ticking louder than ever with no viable prospects. Derek immediately came to mind. He was such a great guy and a wonderful father. It was a shame he refused to give love another try. Even if he wasn't interested in spending a lifetime with her, she wished he wouldn't close himself off to the possibility of remarrying. She couldn't understand why people would intentionally want to live their lives alone. She wasn't giving up on love. And not just any love. She wanted a soul-stirring, toe-curling type of love where passion was at the center of the relationship.

Twenty minutes later, she walked into the house with Jason in her arms and laid him on the sofa. He didn't stir until she reached into the refrigerator for a bottled water.

"I want my daddy," he sobbed, big, fat tears rolling down his cheeks.

Macy's heart swelled. He was such a happy child, and seeing him cry almost made her want to do the same. "Oh, honey, don't cry. Your daddy is at work." She sat next to him. "Ah, c'mere." She lifted him onto her lap. "He'll be here soon. So no crying, okay?" He whimpered as she rocked him, but soon his sobs quieted.

As Jason held Macy around her waist, his curly head resting against her breast, she continued to rock him. This was what she wanted in her life. This was what she was meant to be…a mother.

Hours later, Derek strolled toward his office suite, feeling as if he had gone through the spin cycle of a washing machine. The back-to-back meetings had kicked his butt. He couldn't wait to go home, shower and fall asleep on the sofa.

How pitiful was his life that he was looking forward to hanging out in front of the television? Granted, he would spend some time with Jason, but once he put him to bed, he planned to veg out and be a bum for the rest of the evening.

"Yes, sir, I understand," Louise said to someone on the telephone when he stepped into the office. She lifted a finger to him, signaling for him to give her a minute. "That sounds perfect. I'll make sure I get that information to you." Derek didn't know who she was talking to, but he was amazed at how she could hold a conversation on the phone and type on the computer without missing a beat.

She closed her eyes and grimaced when she hung up the phone.

Derek chuckled, knowing she was probably talking to Mr. Smith. The guy could go on and on without taking a breath. He seemed to be the only person who rattled Louise.

"Dare I ask what that was all about?" Derek moved closer to the desk.

"Don't." She smiled and handed him his messages. "Oh, did you talk to Macy? She was trying to reach you earlier."

Just hearing her name caused a stir in his body. "No. I forgot my cell phone here. I had planned on coming back at lunchtime, but Ted's secretary had brought food in and we ended up having a working lunch. Did Macy say what she wanted?"

"Oh dear. That means you don't know about Jason." Derek was sure his heart stopped. His imagination immediately twisted out of control, thinking the worst had happened. "The school was trying to reach you earlier."

"Is he okay?"

"According to Macy, he is. They called her when they couldn't reach you, and she went to the school and picked—"

"What? He's sick and I didn't know?" Derek turned toward his office to get his cell phone.

"Derek," Louise said with force, stopping him in his tracks, his hand on the doorknob. For a moment she reminded him of his mother, with the authority in her voice. "Jason is fine. He had a stomachache, but Macy assured me he's okay. Remember, she *is* a doctor."

Derek released a breath, as well as the doorknob. For years, it had been just him and Jason. Granted, his family was always there to help out, but never had his son been sick and he not been there.

As if sensing his anxiousness, Louise walked around her desk and touched his arm. "I know you're still adjusting to your new environment and city, but you're not alone." She squeezed his arm and Derek understood more and more every day why Noah spoke so highly of Louise. She had been his mentor's assistant for over fifteen years and Derek hoped she didn't have any plans of retiring anytime soon. "Macy said she's at home with him and to give her a call when you can."

Derek nodded and patted her hand, thinking of her as more than an assistant. "Louise, you're the best."

Moments later, he sat at his desk and called Macy.

"Hello." She answered on the third ring and sounded as if she had been sleeping.

"Hey, baby," he finally said. "I hear you've had some company this afternoon."

She chuckled. "As a matter of fact, there's this cute little guy asleep in my lap." She filled Derek in on the afternoon that he had missed. After some ginger ale and a nap, Jason felt much better.

Derek wasn't sure what to say. He knew Macy was special, but for her to stop what she was doing to tend to his child meant more to him than words could express.

"Macy...I really appreciate your help. Rarely am I far from my cell phone, and I'm sorry you had to drop everything to pick up my kid."

"Trust me, it was no problem. He's such a sweetheart. He had a few moments when he cried for you, but I used my special powers and he was putty in my hands."

Derek laughed, appreciating her sense of humor. He had seen how great she was with kids and had no doubt his son was in good hands. They talked for a few minutes longer and he agreed to pick up dinner for the three of them on his way home.

After disconnecting the call, Derek sat back in his seat. *It's about time you thought about settling down.* Keith's words flitted through his mind. Derek didn't think he was ready for anything serious, but the thought of him and Macy building on their friendship did appeal to him. She was compassionate and generous, and being with her made him forget all that was on his plate these days.

Derek grabbed his phone and briefcase. He would come up with a way to make them both happy, but he had no intention of getting married again.

Macy was startled awake. Sending a sleepy glance around the room, she wondered what woke her until she heard her cell phone vibrating. Glancing down at Jason, whose head was lying in her lap, she eased a pillow under his head and hurried to her phone.

"Hello," she whispered. She stood in the kitchen where she could still look out over the family room where Jason was sleeping.

"Macy, why are you whispering? Is this a bad time?" her sister Janna asked.

"No, this is okay." She told Janna about picking up Jason from school. Macy had a ton of things she should have been doing instead, but she couldn't pull herself away from him. Whenever he whimpered, she was right there to hold and comfort him.

"So you're practicing for when your little ones come along. Does this mean you and Mr. Hottie McNeighbor are getting serious?"

Macy's faith for having that family she wanted was dwindling. She and Derek were getting closer and had been dating for almost two months, but as far as she knew, his feelings on the subject hadn't changed.

"I'm just trying to be a good neighbor and help Derek out."

"I see," she said in that way Macy hated. She knew a dating tip was coming, but Macy wasn't in the mood to hear it.

"So, what did you call me for?"

Janna hesitated. "Okay." She stretched out the word. "I see someone's not in the mood for chatting. That's all right. I called to see why you haven't gone back to Margie's for your last fitting for your evening gown. I was talking to her this morning and she said she hasn't seen or heard from you."

Macy closed her eyes and rubbed her forehead. She had forgotten all about the evening gown. The East Coast Academy of Pediatrics had recently nominated her for Pediatrician of the Year. Surprisingly, she hadn't thought much about the awards banquet.

"I totally forgot. I'll call her when I get off the telephone with you." They talked a few minutes longer until Jason started to stir. She had given him some soup and crackers earlier, which seemed to make him feel better.

A short while later, Derek arrived.

"Hey," Macy said when she opened the door for him. She had finally been able to pull herself out of Jason's grasp again, giving her enough time to freshen up before Derek arrived.

"Hey yourself." He set the bags of food on the table in the foyer and pulled Macy into his arms. "There's something I've wanted to do all day." He lowered his head and captured her lips in a soul-stirring kiss.

She groaned when he palmed her butt and pulled her tighter against his hard body. She didn't think she would ever get used to their tongue aerobics and the way he ignited a flame within her that only burned for him.

"You taste sweeter each time I kiss you," he mumbled against her lips before lifting his head. He placed a kiss on her cheek and kept his arm around her waist as they walked into the family room where Jason was asleep.

"How long has he been out?"

"Off and on for the past few hours. He told me his stomach wasn't hurting anymore, and we watched a little TV before we both dozed off."

Derek sat on the edge of the sofa and ran the back of his fingers down Jason's cheek. Anyone looking in from the outside would be able to tell immediately how much he loved his son. His gentleness, his devotion and his nurturing nature were only a few of the characteristics about him that she found extremely attractive. Her heart fluttered, imagining how it would be if she and Derek were married and he was that loving and gentle with their child.

Tears pricked the back of her eyes and she turned away. She went back to the foyer for the bags of food and hurried into the kitchen. Was she wasting her time with Derek? She had always heard that you can't change a person. Was she willing to settle for just dating him with no lifelong commitment?

"You okay?" She startled when Derek walked up

behind her, wrapping his arms around her waist and placing a kiss on the side of her neck.

"Mmm...yeah, I'm fine." She eased out of his arms. Pulling a beer from the refrigerator, she handed it to him. She grabbed the fixings for a tossed salad to go with the grilled chicken he had purchased from Whole Foods. She felt more than saw him staring at her as she moved around the kitchen.

"I appreciate you picking up Jason from school. I owe you big. I left my phone on my desk, and one meeting ran into another..." His voice trailed off and Macy looked up and met his intense gaze. Diverting her eyes, she pulled out a cutting board and began slicing cucumbers.

"What's wrong?" He halted the hand she was using to cut up the vegetable. Removing the knife, he laid it on the cutting board and turned her to face him.

Macy stared into his eyes and felt as if she was going to cry. The concern and gentleness brimming in his gaze grabbed hold of her heart and wouldn't let go. Somehow she had fallen in love with him and she wasn't sure how or when.

She lowered her eyes, unable to continue meeting his intense ones. He lifted her chin with the pad of his index finger, forcing her to look at him.

"Talk to me." His voice sounded deeper, each word laced with concern. "Did something else happen today? Are you feeling all right?" His hand caressed her cheek. She closed her eyes and leaned into his touch, unable to stop the single tear that now slid from her eye.

"Baby, you're starting to scare me. What is it?" She

dropped her forehead to his shoulder and wrapped her arms around his neck as a few more tears slipped out. "What's wrong?"

She shook her head against his shoulder, not caring that she was probably getting makeup on his shirt. "It's nothing. I think I'm probably just a little tired."

He didn't say anything for the longest time, just held her. The room was quiet except for the low hum of the refrigerator. The smell of grilled chicken permeated the air and she took a deep breath and let it out slowly. Once she got herself together, she lifted her head.

"Come with me." He held her hand and glanced into the family room at Jason. With the open floor plan, from the kitchen they could see into the family room and part of the formal dining room.

Derek led her out onto the back sun porch that had wall-to-wall windows and overlooked part of the backyard. This had been one of the selling features when Macy had decided to purchase the home; she used it as a reading room.

Derek pulled her over to the sitting area that had two indoor-outdoor love seats and a small round table sitting between them. Sitting on one of the love seats, he settled her on his lap. Cradled in his strong arms, she felt so protected…and loved. He hadn't said the words, but she believed…hoped…that the feeling wasn't one-sided. She knew she loved him but had no idea how he felt about her.

With her head against his shoulder, her hand on his chest, she closed her eyes and breathed him in. He always smelled so clean and fresh, like soap, making her want to stay snuggled up to him.

"I know when you're tired, frustrated or when something is bothering you." His voice rumbled in his chest, vibrating against her ear. She opened her eyes but didn't say anything. "Right now, something heavy is on your mind. You know you can trust me with anything."

She nodded. "I know."

"You also know I'm not the most patient person in the world, but for you, I'll practice patience. We can sit here as long as you like."

Macy didn't know how long they sat out on the porch, but she appreciated him giving her an opening to discuss what had been on her mind for a while.

"Spending my afternoon with Jason made me realize how much I want a child. I've always known I wanted to get married and have some babies, but this afternoon the longing for a family hit me a little hard."

Derek took a deep breath in and slowly released it but didn't speak. Macy already knew where he stood on the subject, but she wanted more.

Not wanting their evening to be too uncomfortable discussing the topic further, knowing it would only bring her heartache, she steered the conversation in a different direction.

She raised her head from his shoulder and toyed with the buttons on his dress shirt.

"You know how you said earlier that you owe me?"

He lifted a thick eyebrow, his gaze never veering from her face. "Yeah," he said slowly.

"Well, I've been nominated for an award this Saturday night and I was wondering if you'd be my escort."

The corner of his lips tilted up and a smile spread across his face as he twirled a strand of her hair around his finger.

"So what's the award?"

"Pediatrician of the Year."

His mouth dropped open. "Macy, baby, that's awesome. Why didn't you say something sooner? That's wonderful news."

She shrugged. She was excited about the nomination, but her days and weeks had been so busy she hadn't had much time to really think about it.

"I don't know." She told him about the organization hosting the banquet and the awards program.

He massaged the back of her neck, his gaze steady on her. "I'd love to be your escort. Just give me the details and it's a date."

They both sat in silence, each caught up in their own thoughts. Macy didn't know what else to say. Though she was hungry, she wasn't ready to get up from his lap.

His hand slid down to the middle of her back and he pulled her close, placing a kiss against her temple.

"I heard what you said, or maybe I should say, I understand what you're saying about marriage and kids." He ran his free hand over his mouth and down his chin before letting it fall to her lap. "Baby, you mean so much to me. When we went into this relationship, I told you my position on this. That hasn't changed for me." He turned her face toward his, forcing her to look at him. "I care about you more than I thought I could ever care about a woman again, but I don't know if I can offer you anything more."

Macy traced her finger over his bottom lip and then kissed him. "I know," she said when she pulled back. "I'm not asking for more from you."

He brought her hand to his mouth and kissed the backs of her fingers. "Are you saying you'll be asking for *more* from someone else?"

She shook her head. "No. I'm not saying that." She wasn't interested in anyone else. No one made her feel the things that Derek made her feel. She wasn't expecting more from him because he had already made his position on the subject clear. It was up to her to determine if she would settle for what he offered or whether she would move on. And at the moment, she wasn't sure what she wanted to do about their relationship. "I'm going to go and put dinner on the table."

She tried to climb off his lap, but he held her firm. "I don't want you to think I'm not hearing what you're saying. I understand you want more. I get that." Rubbing her back with slow movements, he chose his next words carefully. "I never thought I'd meet another woman who would come to mean so much to me. Macy, you have brought a certain peace and happiness into Jason's and my lives that I never thought I would ever experience again."

She stared into his eyes and the love Derek saw swimming in her orbs sent heat roaming through his body. He knew she was a special find, but that little twinge of doubt swam around in the back of his mind.

"I want you to have everything you want. I'm just—"

"I know," she said, her soft hands caressing the light scruff covering his cheeks. "I'm not trying to put any pressure on you, but I can't help what's in my heart. I love you and Jas—" She quickly glanced away as if she had said too much. When she tried to stand again, he helped her up. "I'm going to go… I'll be in the kitchen. Jason should be awake soon."

Derek watched as she headed back inside the house. Rubbing his palm down his face, he wasn't sure how he felt about Macy. No. That wasn't true. He cared about her. He just wasn't ready for what she was looking for. *Been there, done that.*

He pushed himself into a standing position. Roaming over to one of the screened windows, he glanced out at the sprawling backyard with its tall evergreen trees framing the perimeter of the lot. The scent of Macy's numerous rosebushes wafted to his nostrils and he breathed in. The tranquil space did nothing to calm the anxiety building within him.

He couldn't do marriage again. The first few months were wonderful. Amazing sex, plenty of laughs, traveling, and he and his ex-wife had basically done everything together. The numerous romantic dinners, bubble baths and all of the laughs came to mind, bringing with them happy memories. When he had committed his life to her, promising to love and cherish her until death, he'd meant it. He had set out to create a marriage and life that dreams were made of, but she had tossed it back into his face.

Derek placed his hands on each side of the window

frame. His stomach churned with the bitter taste of how she had left him. Despite the fact that he'd created the life any woman would love, Sam still walked out without caring that she was leaving him with a small child who needed a mother. It didn't matter that he had a great job, making excellent money. They'd lived in a five-bedroom home in a prestigious area of Cincinnati, where they had planned to have and raise at least three children. Still, it hadn't been enough to make her stay.

He couldn't put himself through that type of hurt again, and now he had Jason to think about. His son was already in love with Macy. If things got any more serious between them and she left, it would break Jason's heart. And his.

"Derek?"

He whipped his head around. Macy stood in the doorway, her sweet face and gentle smile making his heart contract. "Yeah, baby?"

"Come on, let's eat."

"All right, I'll be right there." He watched as she turned to go back in. He could continue to fight his feelings for her if he wanted to, but he already knew. Macy had his heart.

Macy is not your ex. Again, Keith's words shifted around in his mind. Even his brother Craig had told him it was time to stop mourning the loss of his marriage and move on, find love. Everyone expected him to just forget what he'd been through, but hurt and anger still crept in whenever he considered trying love again. The memories were burned in his mind.

He turned from the screened-in porch and headed

for the door that led into the house. Maybe he would just let their relationship play out. If things worked out, fine. If not, he'd enjoy their time together while he could.

Chapter 12

On Saturday night, Derek rang Macy's doorbell, prepared to hear her say that she wasn't ready. He couldn't understand how she could be late all the time for every—

The front door swung open and Derek stood speechless. He always thought Macy was one of the most beautiful women he'd ever met, but tonight she had taken her loveliness to a whole different level. Truly a vision. The sky-blue, off-the-shoulder evening gown left his mouth watering and another part of his body stirring.

"By your expression, you either like what you see or I need to hurry back upstairs and change."

"You're stunning" were the only two words he could manage. She stepped into his arms and immediately his mouth covered hers. His hand cradled the back of her neck and slowly worked its way down to her round butt, giving her firm cheeks a slight squeeze. God, he wanted her. He pulled her closer, letting her feel the effect she had on him. A kiss that had started out gentle quickly turned into one of hunger and need. He hadn't seen her all day and he intended to make up for lost time.

Macy moaned and slowly lifted her head. When she tried to pull away, Derek maintained his hold. "Did I mention that you're absolutely stunning?" he murmured against her lips.

"You might have." She met his gaze and he lost himself in the warmth of her eyes. Tonight, there was something different about her. Or maybe he was the one who was different.

"Maybe we should go upstairs so you can show me what's under this sexy dress before we go."

Macy caressed the back of his head as Derek placed soft kisses against her cheek, working his way down her scented neck. From day one, she'd done wicked things to his self-control, but lately, he couldn't get enough of her.

"And be late? I don't think so." She nudged his chest and stepped out of his arms. Derek moved farther into the house, closing the door behind him. "For the first time since we've been dating, I'm actually ready on time. There is no way I'm going to allow you to make us late." He watched her glide across the room. Her dress hugged her curves perfectly.

He released a long breath and readjusted himself.

She had him so turned on he was tempted to carry her up the stairs and ravish her body, the awards banquet be damned.

She grabbed her shawl and overnight bag. The dinner was at a downtown hotel and they were planning to stay the night. Handing him the bag, she placed a kiss against his cheek.

"I'm ready."

Yeah, me, too, he thought, but knew they weren't talking about the same thing.

"Before we go, I have something for you." He pulled a gift bag from behind his back, the name of the most exclusive jewelry store in the country printed on the outside of it. He had given her a number of gifts over the past few months, yet she squealed and grinned as if this were the first time.

"Derek, you shouldn't have, but I'm really glad you did." She laughed. Seeing the sparkle in her eyes was worth the obscene amount of money he had paid for the items. "Just by the name on the bag, I'm sure you spent way too much for this," she said as if reading his mind.

"You don't even know what it is. How do you know how much I spent? Besides, it's time I started sharing my newfound wealth with those I love."

She glanced up at him at the same time he realized what he'd said, but thankfully, she didn't comment. Instead, the love shining in her pretty brown eyes was almost his undoing. He wanted her to know how he felt, but he couldn't bring himself to form those three important words.

"Thank you." She placed her hand behind his neck

and pulled him close for a kiss, still holding the un-opened square box in her other hand. "I love you, too."

Well, damn. He stood, speechless, staring into her eyes, still unable to say the words she deserved to hear. So much for her not commenting on his slipup.

She released him and returned her attention to the gift. Slowly lifting the hinged lid, she gasped when she finally had it open. "Oh. My. Goodness. Derek." With her mouth gaping, she stared down at the diamond necklace and earring set. The brilliant cut stones, set in white gold, sparkled against the satin interior of the box. "This is absolutely breathtaking." She fingered the diamonds along the necklace before touching the teardrop earrings. "No one has ever given me anything this exquisite."

He removed the box from her hand and set it on the coffee table near where they were standing. "Though I think the jewelry you have on now is beautiful, I'd be honored if you wore this set tonight."

"Of course." She quickly removed her stud earrings and the pendant necklace from around her neck. "I have to tell you, though, I feel as if we should have a bodyguard with us while I'm wearing all this bling." She held her hair up while he clasped the necklace, and then she put on the earrings.

"Nah, you'll be all right." He placed a lingering kiss on her cheek and wrapped his arms around her narrow waist. If it were up to him, they would definitely be late tonight, seeing that he couldn't stop touching her. "I plan to be by your side all evening…and all night."

He suckled the taut skin of her neck and didn't stop until she wiggled out of his grasp.

"No way am I letting you mark my neck up before my big night."

He pulled her back into his arms. "Are you sure we don't have time for a quickie?"

"I'm sure." She gave him a peck on the lips, her hands resting on his chest. "But I must say your offer is very tempting. I'd love to see what you have on under this tuxedo." Her hands moved lower. "You look...and feel so good." She rubbed against his shaft that was straining against the front of his pants, taking him to new lengths.

"If you keep touching me like that, we're never going to get out of here." He groaned and grabbed her hand, stopping it from causing any more damage, while trying like hell to get his body under control.

Why fight it? With the way she was looking at him, desire brimming in her eyes, he knew she was just as turned on as he was. Instead of releasing her hand, he turned it and placed a kiss on the inside of her wrist. Working his way up her arm, he knew the feathery kisses were getting the best of her.

"Derek," she groaned, her defenses weakening. "We...can't."

"Yeah, we can." He backed her up against the nearest wall and ravished her mouth. No other words were spoken as he unzipped her dress and let it fall around her ankles. His hands went first to her waist and then to her breasts. He froze.

Derek lifted his head and quickly took in her appearance. "I can't believe you were going to leave this house with no underwear on," he said roughly, his body tightening as his gaze traveled the length of her perfectly nude body again. The vision of her naked form against the pale blue wall would forever be engrained in his mind.

"I figured I'd make things easy for you after we left the awards banquet." She quickly undid his belt and carefully lowered the zipper on his pants while he dug his wallet out of his pocket. "But now that you've ruined my sur—"

He covered her mouth again, devouring its softness. His thoughts retreated and he was more aware of the heat flowing within him. He wanted her, needed her. Now.

He pulled the foil packet from his wallet and quickly sheathed himself. When she moved away from her dress, he caught her around the waist, not wanting her to move too far. *Foreplay be damned.* He nudged her thighs apart and entered her in one smooth motion.

She gasped. Her arms flew around his neck and she held on, whimpering and groaning with each thrust. His heart pounded and his senses reeled, short-circuiting his brain. God, he loved this woman. Her sweet, sexy sounds were driving him crazy. He hated taking her like this, but he couldn't help it. His control was nonexistent whenever she was near.

"Derek," Macy whimpered, her breathing coming in short spurts, her moves more jerky.

Waves of ecstasy crashed within him and he knew he, too, was teetering on the edge of his release. *Paradise.*

That's what it felt like being deep inside her. He wanted to slow down. He wanted to give every inch of her body the attention it deserved. He wanted to profess his undying love to her. He couldn't. When her body tightened around him, all he could do was hold on and keep them from tumbling to the floor.

"Derek!" Macy's body trembled violently. An orgasm ripped through her with such force, he felt her fingers dig into his shoulder despite the thickness of his jacket.

Unable to hold on, a hot tide of passion roared through him and he came hard with a growl, holding back a curse word when his world spun out of control.

He collapsed against her, clutching her tightly around her waist, his forehead resting against the wall. Their ragged breathing mingled in the quiet of the room. *Intense.* That was the only way to describe what had just happened.

Derek didn't know how long they maintained their position, but he suddenly thought about the time. If they didn't hurry, they were definitely going to be late.

Derek pushed back some, but maintained his hold around her waist. "Okay, we'd better go," he said, still panting. He placed a quick kiss against her lips and patted her hip before he went in the direction of the half bath.

"Oh, so now you're ready to go?" Macy mumbled behind him.

They cleaned up and redressed quickly. When Macy was finished fussing with her hair and makeup, she punched him in the arm.

"If I'm late, you're going to pay."

Derek grinned and pulled her against him, kissing her neck. "I promise. You won't be late, but you can still make me pay afterward if you like."

"Yeah. Whatever." He laughed when she swatted at him and headed for the door.

Two hours later, dinner plates had been cleared, and they were eating dessert—a decadent raspberry cheesecake. Those at Derek and Macy's table included her sisters Janna and Iris, as well as Iris's husband, Nash, Tania, and Rachel and her husband. There were three other people who Macy introduced as friends, but Derek hadn't met them before that evening. The only person missing was Noah. On the way to the hotel, Macy had mentioned how she wished he could have shared the night with them. Not only had Noah been a part of all the highs and lows of his life, but he had also been a part of Macy's, too. So when Macy shed a few tears before they arrived, Derek understood what she felt.

Derek sipped his Scotch. Conversation flowed easily around him, but all he could think about was him and Macy. Was he ready to truly embrace the feelings he was developing for her? His brother had warned him weeks ago that if he wasn't planning to see the relationship all the way through and give Macy that happily-ever-after, he needed to get out immediately. Too late. Derek couldn't let her go even if he wanted to. She held a solid spot in his heart.

As the ceremony neared the last award, Macy's anxiousness didn't go unnoticed. She squirmed in her seat next to Derek, and he was surprised at how nervous she'd been all night. He squeezed her hand and she glanced up at him. He smiled, hoping to help her relax.

"Now, moving along with the program, our last award is for Pediatrician of the Year," the host announced.

"And this year's award goes to…Dr. Macy Carter!"

The room erupted in applause and Derek stood, pulling Macy up with him.

"Ah, baby," he said, gathering her into his arms for a hug and a quick kiss on the lips. "Congratulations!"

"Oh my God," she said, smiling nervously.

"Go on and get your award." Derek nudged her toward the front of the room and joined in clapping with everyone else.

Derek sat listening as Macy gave her acceptance speech. He wasn't surprised that she'd won. From what he'd seen of her compassion and willingness to make her patients her top priority, no one deserved the award more than her. How many times had she received a call in the middle of the night from a parent because their child was sick? What about the number of times she'd had to rush to the hospital because one of her patients was hurt? Derek knew she went beyond the call of duty, and apparently the nominating committee was aware of those things, as well as her contributions and commitments to various charitable organizations.

"I see you haven't been able to take your eyes off my sister since you guys arrived," Janna whispered close to his ear. She had moved to Macy's seat in order to get a better view of the stage.

"She's a very beautiful woman." He spoke without taking his gaze from the podium where Macy was standing.

"I'm glad you two found each other. She deserves some happiness."

Derek nodded and agreed. Macy was always doing things for others, oftentimes putting herself last. He never thought he would ever let a woman near his heart again. Yet somehow Macy had penetrated the wall he had erected.

Derek thought he had been in love with his ex-wife, but what he felt for Macy exceeded anything he had ever felt for Sam. He wasn't sure when it had happened, but Macy had worked her way into his life, as well as his heart. His world was for the better because she was in it.

Chapter 13

"What time is the car supposed to be here?" Macy asked from the hotel bathroom where she was standing in a pink bra and panty set, putting on her makeup. Derek's suggestion to spend the night at the hotel after the awards banquet had been a great idea. After enjoying food, drinks and dancing late into the night, all she had wanted to do was find the nearest bed and fall asleep. Of course, Derek had other plans.

A smile spread across her lips as she recalled their private celebration. Two dozen roses, huge chocolate-covered strawberries and champagne were waiting for her when they made it up to their hotel suite. Derek always made her feel special, but last night had been different. The way his seductive gaze caressed her throughout the evening had her body yearning for his touch. Her heart swelled just thinking about how he had thoroughly worshipped every inch of her body as they made love until the wee hours of the morning.

"The car will be here in about an hour," Derek said, interrupting her thoughts. She lowered the mascara wand and glanced at him over her shoulder as he leaned against the doorjamb. He stood there with his dress shirt hanging open, revealing his muscular chest and rock-hard abs. His pants were zipped, but he hadn't fastened them, nor had he buckled his belt, causing them to hang low on his hips. The man's body was absolute perfection.

Her pulse quickened when the corner of his lips lifted into a flirtatious smile. "I was thinking we could grab lunch before heading home, but then again, the way you're undressing me with your eyes, maybe you have something else in mind." He walked up behind her; placing his hands palm-down on the counter on each side of her, he locked her between his arms.

The lower part of his body ground against her back-side and she shook her head, smiling. "You're insatiable."

"Only when it comes to you."

Macy leaned back against him, loving how good the light kisses he placed along her neck felt. And with a flick of his fingers, he unsnapped the front of her bra, letting it fall open. The straps slid down her arms and she let the lacey garment fall to the floor. The moment Derek cupped her breasts, she knew lunch would have to wait.

"I want you...again," he said, kneading her breasts and tweaking her nipples.

Macy moaned, her body succumbing to his touch as her knees went weak. She gathered what little strength she had and turned to face him. She wanted him, too. As she ran her hands up his smooth chest, his muscles rippled beneath her touch when she relieved him of his shirt. His pants were next, but he stopped her when he lowered his head and claimed her lips, crushing her to him.

Derek groaned against her mouth and palmed her butt. "Let's take this to the bed." He lifted her with ease and carried her into the room, laying her in the center of the mattress. "I love the pink lace, but these have to go," he said of her panties as he slid them down her legs. He appraised her with unabashed interest and a shiver stirred through her body.

God, she loved this man. She had no idea what the future held for them, but every day they spent in each other's presence, she became more and more excited about the possibility of them spending the rest of their lives together.

Derek stood and dug into his pocket for his wallet, removing a condom. He laid it on the bedside table and stepped out of his pants before climbing on the bed.

"I can't seem to get enough of you." His tongue explored the dark peaks of her breasts, stroking and licking her sensitive nipples. Macy didn't think she would ever get enough of him, either. Each time they made love felt like the first time. Like an exciting new experience.

Derek's hand skimmed over her stomach and eased between her thighs. Macy knew this round of sex would be quick because already a vehement pressure built within her. He slid one skilled finger between her slick folds and then another. Warmth flowed through her body like hot lava down a rocky mountain, burning everything in its path as he glided in and out of her heat.

"Derek," she gasped in sweet agony, catching the rhythm of his fingers and moving roughly against his hand. Passion pounded blood through her veins and she breathed in deeply when he picked up speed. Her body moved of its own accord and she gripped his biceps, trying to hold on.

Derek showed no mercy. He increased the pace and the pressure. Macy lost it. Her head thrashed back and forth against the pillow and she bucked against his hand, her nails digging into his skin. A deluge of fiery sensations erupted through her body when her release ripped through her with explosive proportions. It was as if she were suspended in the air with nothing to hold on to before her body collapsed. Panting hard, she lay sated and watched him through the narrow slits of her eyes as he quickly sheathed himself.

Derek returned to the bed and kissed her tenderly. "You can't give out on me yet. We're just getting started."

He buried himself in her and Macy's body responded immediately, tightening around his thick shaft. His gaze met hers as he began to rotate his hips. The love she saw brimming in his eyes drew her to a height of fervor she had never felt with him before. There was no doubt in her mind that he was hers, and she was his.

Still rocking his body, Derek lowered his head and reclaimed her lips without missing a beat. She loved this man with everything in her and she wanted to scream to the world, *He's mine*! In her heart, she knew that he was the man she would spend the rest of her life with.

Derek moaned and pulled his mouth from hers. His thrusts became more erratic, his breathing more labored, as he pumped in and out of her.

"Macy." He stretched her name out and he slammed into her, going deeper, faster and harder. She clung to his shoulders. Her body thrummed as a climax built within her. "Ma…cy!" he growled with a final thrust and she shattered around him. His body jerked uncontrollably upon his release and he gritted his teeth. He spewed a curse just as his arms buckled and his body went limp on top of her.

Seconds ticked by before he lifted slightly and rolled onto his back, pulling Macy against his sweat-slicked body. Neither of them spoke. Their heavy breathing mingled, filling the quietness of the room, and Macy lay satiated, loving the feel of being wrapped in Derek's strong arms. She closed her eyes and savored what they had just shared. She was right where she wanted to be.

"I love you so damn much," Derek whispered against her ear.

Macy's eyes popped open. She wasn't sure if he thought she had fallen asleep, but she said nothing. It was the first time he'd spoken those words that she longed to hear. And he had said them with such authority.

She smiled and closed her eyes again, basking in the knowledge of knowing that her feelings for him weren't one-sided.

I love you, too.

Derek knew he was still walking around with a stupid grin on his face as he recalled his weekend with Macy. He couldn't help it. Just thinking about her stirred a desire within him that he found hard to contain.

"Good morning, Derek, I'm glad you're here," Louise said when he stepped into the office.

"Good morning. What's going on?"

"Joel just called and said they're having a problem with the Orlando project. Your first meeting is not for another hour. Do you have time to meet with him first?"

"Yeah, have him come up."

Gone were the days of Derek creating a schedule and sticking to it. Since he'd begun his new role at Price, it seemed his schedule changed constantly. At first, it had made him anxious when the day went in a different direction than planned. He hadn't realized just how rigid he had been until Macy had pointed it out. Her exact words were, "You need to loosen up and just go with the flow sometimes."

A smile found its way to his lips, thinking about her again. They were like night and day, and she definitely balanced him.

A light knock caught his attention. "Can I come in?" Joel stood in the open doorway.

"Sure, come in. We can sit at the table." Joel followed him to the round table and opened his laptop.

"Sorry to bother you first thing this morning, but we have something of an emergency."

Joel pulled up a set of plans on his Mac computer and caught Derek up on the multimillion-dollar Orlando project. Derek had worked with some amazing architects over the years. Yet he was impressed by the level of young architects at the firm like Joel, who were newly out of college and had some fresh, innovative ideas.

"We are three months into the plans and every time we get close to finalizing them, the client wants something changed." Joel sat back in his seat. "I think if you can attend the next face-to-face meeting with them, maybe we can hash out the differences and finalize everything."

"When is the next one?"

"Tomorrow morning."

Thanks to having a company jet, Derek wouldn't have a problem flying out in the morning and then returning late afternoon or early evening. And thankfully Jason's transportation to and from school was taken care of. He had partnered with a couple of the parents in the neighborhood to offer a carpool for those children who attended the same preschool program as Jason. His son was covered for the next three days. The only thing he needed to make sure of was whether or not Keith was going home right after work, or if they needed to see about Jason staying at his little friend's house until Derek arrived home.

"Joel, let me check on some things and I'll get back to you shortly."

They talked for a few minutes longer before Joel left the office. Derek glanced at his schedule for the next day. He could postpone his morning meetings, but he had a major meeting late afternoon that he couldn't reschedule.

He stood and grabbed the file that he would need for his next meeting. Juggling his son and work wasn't always easy, but Derek felt good in knowing that he had a support system in place.

He pocketed his cell phone and whistled as he left his office. His life in Atlanta was turning out better than he could have ever imagined. He knew part of the reason for the peace he felt had to do with Macy. He was glad she hadn't mentioned anything more about marriage and kids. Maybe they were finally on the same page. He was confident that they could have a great relationship without adding those to the mix.

Macy left the clinic and hurried to her car. The moment she climbed in, her cell phone rang. *I'm never going to get anything done if this phone keeps ringing.* She started the car and activated her Bluetooth.

"Hello?"

"So, Ms. Busy Woman, how's it going?" Iris asked, her voice coming in loud and clear inside the car. "I haven't heard from you since the banquet. Are you avoiding me?"

"Iris, are you serious? That was what, three days ago? You act as if we haven't talked in months."

"Oh, well, it seems longer, especially since we usually talk every day."

"I know, but things have been crazy busy," she said as she pulled onto the highway. "I had a board meeting at the children's hospital earlier that ran over, and it has thrown my schedule off. Now I have to go meet with Noah's lawyer about a couple of things, and then I need to go grocery shopping because I'm cooking dinner for Derek and Jason tonight." Her gaze drifted to the clock on the dashboard. "Oh, shoot, that reminds me—I need to make sure I remember to pick up the buns and tablecloths for the cookout this weekend."

"Macy, sis, you're doing too much. When are you going to slow down?"

Anger singed Macy's last nerve. "I'll slow down when you and everyone else I know stop asking so much of me!" she snapped. She couldn't believe Iris, of all people, was telling her she needed to slow down. When Iris's doctor had told her she was going to have to take it easy while pregnant, Macy had stepped in to help, running small errands for her here and there. Between that and the requests for favors from others, Macy wanted to scream, "Enough!"

When the silence on the other end of the phone got to be too much, Macy sighed. It wasn't Iris's problem that Macy had a hard time juggling her schedule and saying no to her family and friends.

"I'm sorry. I didn't mean to snap at you."

"No. I'm the one who should be apologizing. I can

easily hire a personal assistant to do some of the things I've been asking you to help with lately. I wish I had thought to do that in the first place. No, on second thought, I wish you would have just said no."

Macy exited the highway, only to fall in line with hundreds of other drivers trying to turn left on Roswell Road. "You're right. I should have said something. But the things I do for you and others, I want to do. I think, with my workload, and the medical complex renovations and everything else, my life has just spun a little out of control."

The part of her life that was going great, though, was Derek. Just thinking about him sent a warm, fuzzy feeling flowing through her body. After this past weekend, it finally felt as if their relationship was heading in the right direction. She smiled at the thought that she might actually get her happily-ever-after.

"Well, don't worry about the things for the cookout." Iris's voice cut into her thoughts. "I'll get Tania or Nash to pick those items up. And when you get a chance to breathe, shoot me a text or an email and let me know what else I can take off your plate. There's no reason why you should be doing everything."

Macy smiled and released a breath as she sped up to catch the green light. She didn't know what she would do without her sisters. They drove her nuts sometimes, but they were always there for her.

"I think I can…" She gasped and stepped on the gas when she noticed a car come out of nowhere, barreling toward her driver's-side door. She gripped the steering wheel and braced herself when it seemed she wouldn't be able to get out of the way fast enough. "Oh God... *Aaarghhhh*," she screamed as metal crushed around her.

"Macy? Macy!"

Macy heard her name but couldn't respond. Searing pain shot through her left arm. Tears filled her eyes. She couldn't move. Sounds drew fainter and the agonizing pressure in her head became unbearable. Visions of her sisters, Jason and Derek flitted around in her mind. Derek. *God, please don't let me die before I get my happily-ever-after* was her last thought as everything went black.

Derek sat at the long conference room table, trying to stay focused as his CFO explained why two projects were over budget. His day had started at five in the morning. Besides the downtime he'd had on the hour-long flight to and from Orlando, he hadn't taken much of a break. Exhaustion crept in. Exhaustion and hunger weren't a good combination, especially when he was sitting in a meeting where finances were being discussed.

He had arrived back in town a couple of hours earlier and was now on his second meeting. If he hadn't needed to know how they were going to get back on track with these jobs, Derek would have postponed this one.

"Excuse me." Derek looked up to see Louise at the door. "I'm sorry to interrupt, but Derek, may I speak to you for a minute?"

He excused himself and followed his assistant out

of the room, shutting the door behind him. "What's up, Louise?" She had never pulled him out of a meeting before.

"There's been an accident."

Jason. Fear like nothing Derek had ever experienced chilled the blood running through his veins. If anything had happened to...

"Where is he?" Derek turned and practically ran to his office for his car keys. "Where's my son, Louise?"

"Derek, please. Stop!" she said when she caught up to him in his office. "It's not Jason. It's Macy."

Derek gripped the edge of his desk. It was as if someone had punched him in the gut, knocking the air out of him.

"What's happened?"

"Iris called. Macy was in a car accident. It's bad."

"Is she..." The words lodged in his throat and air into his lungs wasn't coming easily. He honestly didn't know what he would do if something had happened to her.

"She's in the hospital. Iris didn't know much yet, but she said that Macy has been in and out of consciousness."

"I have to go to her," he mumbled, looking on his desk and in his briefcase for his keys. It wasn't until Louise touched his arm that he remembered that he kept them in the top drawer of his desk. "Can you let those in the meeting know...I need to go?" He started for the office door, but Louise stopped him again.

"Derek, you can't drive like this. Sit down. I'll contact the car service."

Chapter 14

Derek hurried down the hallway, following the instructions the hospital staff had given him to get to Macy's room. While he'd been sitting in traffic for the past forty-five minutes, his mind had taken him on a wild ride of what-ifs. What if she was seriously hurt? What if he lost her? According to an update from Iris, Macy was okay, but that didn't stop him from imagining the worst.

He made the last turn down the hallway and passed two closed doors on his right before he arrived at Macy's room. Taking a deep breath and letting it out slowly, he pushed the door open.

Iris and Tania glanced up when he walked in.

"How is she?" he asked, hugging them both and not missing their tearstained faces.

When he directed his attention to the body that lay motionless on the bed, Derek's chest tightened. Macy might have been sleeping, but seeing her lying so still sent a wave of uneasiness through him.

She has to be all right.

His gaze traveled from the large bandage on the side of her head down to the long eyelashes brushing her high cheekbones. She looked so tiny. The pained expression on her face didn't sit well with him. He needed to know what exactly had happened and why his woman was lying in a hospital hooked up to an IV and with a cast on her left arm.

"According to the doctors, she's going to be fine." Iris stood on the opposite side of the bed, her hand moving slowly up and down Macy's arm. Derek wasn't sure if the gesture was to comfort Macy or Iris herself. "He said she was very lucky, but they want to keep her under observation for the next twenty-four hours."

"Then she can go home?" Derek asked. When Iris nodded, he returned his attention to Macy, who hadn't stirred.

"She has a mild concussion and a few bumps and bruises," Tania added when she moved to stand next to Iris. "She was awake a little while ago and asked about you."

"I told her that I had called your office and that you were on your way. Despite trying to stay awake, she drifted back to sleep," Iris said.

Derek leaned over the bed. Frustration gnawed at him, knowing that there wasn't anything he could do for Macy. He brushed some of her hair away from her forehead and caressed her cheek with the back of his fingers, studying her beautiful face. She had been perfectly fine the day before and now here she was, laid up in a damn hospital bed.

"Baby, I need you to get well," he whispered, and placed a lingering kiss on her lips.

Derek stood and swallowed hard, unable to pull his gaze from her. Part of him wanted to hold her tight and never let her go, but there was another emotion warring within him. A deep-seated emotion that he hadn't felt in a long time before today. Fear. Fear of loving someone so much that he'd felt as if he would die without them. Other than Jason, Derek had only experienced these feelings for one other person: his ex-wife, Samantha.

The thought shook him and he abruptly took a step back from the bed. He had promised himself that he would never subject himself to that type of vulnerability. He would never allow another woman to get that close to his heart. He had loved and lost once. He couldn't go through that again. He couldn't suffer through that type of pain. Yet he had allowed himself to fall in love...again.

I can't do this. I can't...

Derek backed farther away from the bed, rubbing his chest, finding it hard to breathe.

"Derek?" Iris walked to his side and placed her hand on his back. "Are you okay?"

"Yeah. Yeah, I'm... I'm fine."

"You don't look fine. Do you need a doctor?"

Derek shook his head. "Air. I just need some air." He pulled away from her and hurried to the door, but then stopped. He had one hand on the handle and the other on his chest, where his heart felt as if it would leap right out of his body. "When Macy wakes up, tell her that I was here and that I'll be back."

Derek pulled open the door and walked out. He didn't know where he was going, but he knew he had to get the hell out of there. He needed to think. Something he clearly hadn't been doing for the past few months. Otherwise, he wouldn't have let this happen. He wouldn't have let Macy break through the barrier he had placed securely around his heart.

Macy watched Derek as he moved around her kitchen tidying up. He was truly the total package. Good-looking, sexy and he could cook. What more could a girl ask for?

Actually, there was more she wanted. For the past two weeks he'd been keeping his distance, claiming she was still healing. The doctor had given her a clean bill of health. Emotionally, riding in a car still made her uncomfortable, but outside of the cast that she had to wear for the next four weeks, she felt fine. And what she wanted more than anything right now was to lead Derek to her bedroom and make mad, passionate love.

He dried his hands and turned off the lights in the kitchen. As he made his way into the family room, she stood from the sofa. She unbuttoned her shirt, allowing it to slide down her arms and onto the floor. If he wouldn't make the first move, then it was up to her.

He stopped in his tracks. His gaze took in her royal blue lacy bra and traveled down to her hand as she slipped her fingers into her waistband and pushed her yoga pants down. Desire showed in his gorgeous brown eyes and he gulped. Macy almost burst out laughing. He looked as if this was going to be their first time.

But then her smile slipped from her lips. She could feel his tension—or was it anxiousness?—from across the room. The desire she had first seen in his eyes now looked more like fear. *Something's not right.* She slid her pants back up over her hips.

"Derek, what's going on? And don't you dare tell me nothing. You've been acting strange for weeks and I want to know why."

He lowered his gaze, ran his hand over his head and walked farther into the family room. Instead of reaching for Macy as he usually did, he moved past her and dropped down in the upholstered chair next to the sofa.

Something is definitely wrong.

Macy stooped and picked up her shirt, slipping back into it. She tried to remain calm, but a sense of foreboding gripped her, sending her imagination all over the place.

"Please tell me what's going on." She sat in the far corner of the sofa, as if being next to him would be bad for her health.

Derek leaned forward in his chair, his elbows on his thighs. He released a long, frustrated growl that only made Macy more anxious. Whatever he had to tell her was bad. Very bad.

As he rubbed his forehead with both hands, unease ran down Macy's spine. Now she wasn't so sure she wanted to know what was bothering him.

"Where do you see yourself five years from now?" he asked.

That intense gaze he'd worn like a shield when they'd first met showed in his eyes. Macy didn't know where this question was going, but she had a good idea. Actually, it was one she should have been asking him.

"In five years, the medical complex, named after Noah, will be fully operating with specialists in at least twenty fields under one roof. I also see myself married to an amazing man with at least one child and another on the way. What about you, Derek? Where do you see yourself in five years?"

Macy knew she should only ask a question that she was ready to hear the answer to, but it was time. It was time she found out for sure if she and Derek were on the same page. Sure, in some cases, actions spoke louder than words, but today she needed to hear his words. The past few months with him had been wonderful, giving her hope that they would one day be husband and wife. Now she needed to know if he could see himself married...married to her.

"I'm not sure," he said without making eye contact, which was a first. "A year ago, I was sure what I wanted, and I was sure I knew the direction my life was going." He looked up and met her gaze.

Macy didn't know what to say. That wasn't the response she was expecting, nor was it the one she'd hoped for.

"The one thing I do know is that I love you. You're wonderful, and I never thought I'd be able to love another woman again after the way Sam left."

Joy bubbled inside Macy. Maybe they really were on the same page. Maybe Derek would be a part of her happily-ever-after.

"Though I love you, I think we should just be friends. Macy, I know I can't give you what you want. What you deserve. And you deserve everything your heart desires."

Macy could only stare at him. No words formed in her mouth because her brain went temporarily blank. How does one go from being in love with someone to only wanting to be friends?

"When we started seeing each other, I made it clear that I wasn't looking for anything serious. Through no fault of your own, our relationship has gone in a direction that I hadn't intended...and I can't do this anymore."

"You can't do what anymore? Lead me on? Make me believe that you love me and that I mean something to you?"

"I do care about you, Macy, and I didn't try to lead you on. I've done the marriage thing already and—"

"Derek, I'm not your ex! And I'm getting sick and tired of you making me pay for something she did." Anger dripped from each word. "She left! Get over it! Move on with your life and quit using what she did to keep me at bay. You either want to have a life with me or you don't. It's that simple." Emotion clogged her throat and she stood. Walking to the other side of the room, she leaned against the fireplace mantel.

Derek stood also, but kept his distance. "Baby, I love being with you. I'm just not ready for what you're ready for, but it doesn't mean that you're not important to me. Because you are, and I do love you."

Macy heard the words and the emotion behind them, but she wasn't sure if she believed them anymore. How could she? One minute he was professing his love to her, and the next he was suggesting they just be friends.

"So all of a sudden you realize that you love me, but we can't be more than friends. How is that possible?"

Derek's brows drew together. "What do you mean?"

Macy tilted her head. "What do you mean, what do I mean? How can you say you love me? How can you love someone or be friends with them if you clearly don't trust them?"

"What? You know I trust you."

"No, I don't! The man I love more than life is afraid to take a chance on me. Afraid to trust that I would never walk out on him the way his ex-wife did." She started toward him but stopped herself. If she got any closer, there was no telling what she would do to him. "You hurt me. You made me believe in us, made me believe that there was a chance for us to be together… forever." Her hand rested against her heart. "There is nothing, and I mean absolutely *nothing*, I wouldn't do for you or Jason. The fact you could think that I would or could just walk away from either of you breaks my heart."

"Macy, baby, I'm sorry. I never meant to hurt you. I—"

"Get out." Her voice might have been low, but there was no doubt in her tone that she wanted him to leave.

Derek leaned back as if she had struck him. "What? You don't mean—"

"Get out of my house!"

He didn't move.

Macy stomped to the front door and pulled it open. "Now!"

Derek hesitated, but eventually grabbed his keys from the kitchen counter and moved toward her.

"Baby, don't do this. We—"

"Derek…just leave."

When he finally walked out, she closed the door behind him and leaned against it. She slid to the floor and covered her face with her hands.

"How could I have been so stupid to think that I could change him?' she sobbed into the quietness of the foyer. She had no one to blame but herself. She knew better than anyone that you couldn't change a man, yet she had hoped. She had hoped that just maybe he could see how good they were together and leave his past experience in the past. "Never again! Never will I settle for less than I deserve."

Derek stormed into the house and slammed the door behind him. At the moment, he didn't care who he woke up. All he could think about was the hurt in Macy's eyes and how he probably should have handled the conversation differently.

Keith seemed to come out of nowhere. "What the hell is wrong with you, slamming the door like that, especially knowing that Jason is asleep?"

"I screwed up." Derek didn't move from his spot in the foyer. He told his brother about the conversation with Macy and how she had kicked him out of her house.

Keith shook his head and walked away. Derek followed him, not able to hear his brother's mumblings. Although he really didn't need to hear them. He was pretty sure Keith was calling him all kinds of idiotic.

"Just say whatever you have to say, Keith." Derek stopped at one of the bar stools and leaned against the back of it. He knew she wouldn't be happy, but he hadn't thought she would kick him out of her house. They'd had similar conversations before and she always said that she understood and respected his position. So her reaction tonight was unexpected. Maybe he shouldn't have added the part about them being friends.

"For a person who is supposed to be so smart, you sure do stupid stuff. I'm starting to think you intentionally sabotaged this relationship." He yanked open the pantry door but peered around it. "Sometimes I think there is no way we can be related."

Derek didn't respond. He hated that he had led Macy on when all the while he knew he couldn't do the marriage thing again, especially when he knew that was what she wanted. After dating for a few months, he thought that maybe she would be okay with a fling.

They were great together. He had only asked her the question about her five-year plan because he had hoped she had given up the idea of being married and having children. In hindsight, maybe it had been a foolish move on his part.

"I didn't intentionally ruin our relationship. I had hoped that she had gotten past the getting-married-and-having-kids idea. I thought we could just keep going along the way we were, but I knew she still wanted more, and I had to be honest with her."

"You're so busy talking about being honest with her that you're missing the fact that you still have trust issues."

"I *had* trust issues. I don't anymore."

Keith pulled out a bag of chips and slammed the door. "How can you say that with a straight face? You just broke up with a phenomenal woman who loved you despite your hang-ups and insecurities. For a minute there, I thought you had put your past behind you and stopped obsessing about the way Sam left, but I guess you haven't."

"I have."

"No, you haven't. What I don't understand is, why now? Why did this come up now after months of going along great?"

"I just told you. She still wanted more than I was ready to give."

Keith shook his head. "Nah, it's something else. It's like you were trying to break up with her, but why? And don't lie. I've known you longer than you've known yourself and can tell when you're lying."

Derek ignored his brother's last statement. Keith was older and had often made similar comments. But his brother was right about one thing. He had intentionally broken up with Macy; he just thought it would go differently.

Ever since the day Derek had visited Macy in the hospital, something inside him had changed. Yes, he still loved her more than words could ever express, but that fear of her someday leaving him had become almost suffocating. Deep in his heart, he knew Macy was nothing like Samantha, but he couldn't get his mind to cooperate with his heart.

"What you should have done was talked to me before you got stupid and broke up with her. I would have told you it was idiotic."

It might not have been his brightest idea, but Derek knew he had done the right thing. He didn't want to hurt Macy any more than he already had.

"So now what are you going to do?"

Derek shrugged. "I'm going to be the best damn CEO I can while I raise my child to be an upstanding citizen."

"And?"

"And I'm going to live with my decision about Macy."

Keith shook his head. "Oh, this ought to be good. I'll give you a week before you're on her doorstep begging for another chance," he mumbled on his way out of the kitchen.

Rarely did Derek go back on a decision and he was confident that breaking up with Macy at this stage in their relationship had to be done.

* * *

The next morning, Derek showed up at Macy's front door an hour before he knew she'd be heading to work. He couldn't stay away. During his sleepless night, he realized that no matter how he tried to fight his feelings, he had to quit lying to himself. Macy was a part of him. Fear of eventually losing her had made him walk away from the woman he wanted. The woman he needed. All night he had berated himself for not being stronger. He loved her. He had to trust that their love would stand the test of time.

Derek tossed thoughts around in his mind, deciding what exactly he would say to her. He hated to admit it, but Keith had been right. Breaking things off with Macy had been the stupidest thing he'd ever done. Derek didn't know why he thought he could live his life without her in it. He had to fix this. She was his heart.

The front door flew open minutes after he rang the bell.

"What are you doing here?" Macy asked. Gone was the smile she usually greeted him with, and instead her brows drew together. He was pretty sure requesting one of her sweet kisses was out of the question. "Derek?" she practically growled.

Derek felt like crap. It was because of him that her eyes were puffy and red, her shoulders slumped and exhaustion seeped from her pores.

"We need to talk," he finally said, thinking a formal greeting would get him a closed door in the face.

"There's nothing else for us to talk about." She folded her arms across her midsection, her cast standing out like a neon sign reminding him of her car accident. "I thought I made that clear yesterday when you reminded me that we didn't want the same thing. I finally get it. At some point, maybe we can be friends, but right now I can't."

"I might have been wrong." Derek moved closer, his free hand gripping the doorjamb. "Give me a chance to explain."

"Derek, I'm on my way to work. I really don't have time for this right now." Since being off work for over two weeks after her accident, she was anxious to get back to "her kids," as she referred to her patients.

"Okay, then, have dinner with me."

On a sigh, her gaze darted around at everything but him before it landed on him again. The sadness in her eyes was almost his undoing. "I can't." Her words were spoken so softly he almost missed them.

Maybe coming here before she headed to work wasn't a good idea.

"Sweetheart, I'm not trying to upset you, but we have to talk about this. I do love you. I know I messed up, but I want to fix this."

She blew out a breath and batted her eyes rapidly to ward off the tears. "I'm sorry, but I just can't do this right now." She stepped back and he let her close the door without trying to stop her.

Heading across the yard to his house, he was more determined than ever to win her back. He would never let fear dictate any aspect of his life again. Now he just had to figure out how to win back the woman he loved.

* * *

"We're done." Macy said to her sister and dabbed at her eyes, feeling like the dumbest woman alive. "He told me more than once he wasn't interested in a serious relationship. I knew he hadn't gotten over his ex leaving the way she had. And I thought I could change him. I thought we really had something. God, how could I have been so stupid?"

"Honey, you're not stupid. You and Derek do have something special." Iris, barely able to move with her protruding stomach, scooted closer to her on the sofa and reached for Macy's hand. "I saw the way he looked at you at the awards banquet and at the hospital. He loves you. It was written all over his face."

"If he loved me so much, why can't he make a lifelong commitment to me? He knows I would never do anything to hurt him. And he knows my heart." She pointed to her chest.

They sat in silence. The only sound was Macy sniffling. She shouldn't be wasting perfectly good tears on him, but she couldn't help it. Never had her heart ached the way it had in the last couple of days. Even returning to work and seeing her kids hadn't helped her mood.

"Macy, I know you're hurt right now. Give it some time. Try to see things from his perspective."

No matter how hard she tried, she couldn't wrap her brain around his point of view. How could he have such little faith in her? All that they had shared over the past few months apparently meant nothing.

Macy sat forward and picked up her half-eaten peanut butter and jelly sandwich, the perfect cure for a broken heart. Taking a bite, she set it back on the small plate.

"Are you sure that salad is enough for you?" Macy asked Iris.

Nash had dropped Iris off at Macy's house on the way to one of his nightclubs. He claimed he thought Macy needed the company, but Macy had a feeling her brother-in-law was afraid his wife would go into labor at any moment, and he didn't want her to be alone while he was busy working.

"It's more than enough. I feel as if all I've been doing is eating." Iris took a swig from her water. "I know you don't want to hear this, but I think you should fight for Derek. You're upset, which is understandable. But I think you two can work through this."

Macy released a frustrated breath and stood. She really didn't want to talk about it anymore.

"Do you remember when I showed up at your house soaking wet, crying because I thought Nash was in love with his crazy ex?" Iris asked.

How could Macy forget? She was worried sick when Nash called her, frantic that Iris had caught him with his ex-girlfriend and then taken off. It was one of the worst rainstorms Atlanta had ever had and Macy was scared to death that Iris had been in an accident.

"I remember."

"Well, you saw how I had everything all wrong. And how I didn't give Nash a chance to explain what was really going on in his office."

"Iris, that was different. Eve was a psycho and everyone who knew you and Nash saw he was madly in love with you. You're the only person who couldn't seem to really see that."

"It's not different."

Macy turned and frowned at her sister. "It *is* different," she growled.

Iris, an attorney, could argue about anything and make one of her stupid ideas or suggestions seem plausible. But there was no way their situations were anywhere close to being the same.

"When Nash and I first started hanging out, he had no intention of ever falling in love. As a matter of fact, he only intended to have an affair with me." She smiled at Macy's shocked expression. "He later told me that piece of information. At any rate, things between us changed. I don't know how or when, but they did and we fell in love. Yet with my insecurities, I struggled with believing he could love someone like me." Her sister released a long sigh and rubbed her hands on her belly, no doubt trying to settle her active twins down. She eventually returned her gaze to Macy. "Like Derek, Nash was caught off guard with his feelings for me, and fear made him doubt what we shared."

Macy retook her seat on the sofa. Okay maybe their situations were similar.

"I probably could go on and on regarding the similarities. But I think the biggest one is how, like Nash, despite his own fears, Derek has not only told you how much he loves you, but he has shown you, as well. Yeah, he might still have a few abandonment issues, but the love you two have for each other can get you both past that. Don't give up on him yet. Don't give up on love."

Macy hated when her sister presented a good argument. She so wanted to disagree with her, but she couldn't. Not totally.

Chapter 15

Macy strolled down the clinic's hallway, jotting notes into her iPad. This had been one of her long days and she couldn't wait to go home. Back at work for a week, she was starting to think that maybe she should have given herself a little more recovery time. She wasn't in pain, but her energy level wasn't back to normal.

Driving was another story. The car service Derek had hired was very dependable, considering she still wasn't ready to get behind the wheel. And when she tried canceling the service, they denied her. They were given strict instructions to be available to her until Derek said otherwise. The only way she could cancel was by going through Derek, and she still wasn't ready to talk to him. Well, she wanted to talk to him, or at least see him, but he had hurt her so badly she didn't know if she would ever get over the pain.

"Hanging in there?" Rachel asked when she came out of one of the exam rooms. She tucked her tablet under her arm and shoved her hands into the pockets of her white jacket.

Macy stopped and wiggled her fingers and arm, hoping to eliminate the itching beneath her cast. "Yeah, although I can't wait to get this thing off. I'm going to be even more sympathetic to my patients who are in casts. It's awful." She glanced down at the cast that was covered with pictures and her patients' names. Her first week back and all the children wanted to write on it or, in some cases, draw on it. She had started carrying around markers with her, encouraging their signatures.

"I can't even imagine how uncomfortable that thing is as an adult. I had one in middle school and it was cool to have for a while, but after six weeks, I was about ready to take it off myself."

They laughed.

"Dr. Carter?"

Macy glanced down the hallway to see their receptionist walking toward them.

"Hi," Cindy said. "Are you able to see one more patient before you head out for the day?"

Macy slumped against the wall and pouted. She loved her job and couldn't think of anything else in the world she'd want to do for a living, but on days like today, she wanted to run for the hills and hide.

"It's Jason Logan," Cindy added, giving Macy a sympathetic look. "His dad brought him in."

"Oh my God." Her heart slammed against her chest, wondering what was wrong with Jason. Thoughts of her cast were all but gone. She hurried to the front of the building with Cindy hot on her heels.

"I knew you would want to see him, but I wasn't sure if I should put him in one of the exam rooms or—"

"No. No. I'm glad you came to get me." She walked into the waiting room and her heart stuttered. The concern on Derek's face made her even more nervous. He held Jason in his arms, but Macy couldn't see Jason's face.

"What's going on?" She hurried toward Derek, placing her hand on Jason's back. "Follow me." She led them to one of the exam rooms.

"I'm sorry to just drop by, but—"

Macy shook her head. "No, no, I'm glad you did." She reached for Jason, who lifted his head from Derek's shoulder and gave her a weak smile. "Hey, sweetheart. What's going on?" She sat in the rolling chair with him on her lap. She hadn't seen him in almost a week and she couldn't stop herself from kissing him and holding him close.

Jason wrapped his arms around her neck and laid his head on her shoulder. "I miss you," he mumbled against her neck. He felt so good in her arms that she never wanted to let him go.

"I'm sorry if we had you worried that something was wrong with him, but he insisted on seeing you. Actually, I needed to see you, too."

When she'd broken up with Derek, it was as if she

had lost a part of her heart. She missed them both something terrible.

Instead of addressing Derek, she squeezed Jason in her arms and kissed him on the cheek. "I've missed you, too," she whispered against Jason's ear. Though she missed them both, she wasn't ready to say it to Derek.

"I know you're still mad at me, and you have every right to be, but we need to talk." Derek moved away from the door and inched toward her. "Please. Just hear me out."

"We have nothing to discuss, Derek. You've already made yourself perfectly clear. We don't want the same things."

Macy placed Jason on his feet and stood. "Come on, Jason. I think I have some snacks in my office." She started for the door, but Derek stopped her with a hand on her arm. He held on to her with one hand and opened the door with the other. Surprised, Macy saw Rachel standing outside the door with a sheepish grin on her face.

They set me up.

"I'm sorry," she mouthed, and escorted Jason out of the room.

"Baby, I'm sorry for showing up like this. I didn't know what else to do. You haven't been answering your telephone, and I've stopped by your house every day, but you haven't been answering the door, either."

Derek pulled Macy into his arms the moment Rachel closed the door. Though her mind shouted for her to put some distance between them, her heart wouldn't let her.

"Before Jason told me how much he was missing you, I had thought about making some picket signs. I was going to camp outside your house and in front of the clinic to beg for your forgiveness and for another chance."

Macy hated to admit how good it felt to be in his arms. She wanted so badly to give him another chance, but that little nettlesome voice in the back of her head said to tread carefully.

She laid her forehead against his hard chest, soaking up his scent and warmth, debating what to tell him. The conversation with Iris a week ago came to the forefront of her mind. Yes, she loved Derek, and deep in her heart she knew he loved her, too. She wanted to spend the rest of her life with him, but was he ready?

Macy lifted her head. "Derek, God knows I love you, but I'm not convinced that you're ready to leave your past in the past. I'm not your ex-wife. I would never treat you the way she did, but I don't want to pay for what she did. I don't want to get hurt." She fiddled with the buttons on his shirt.

He placed his finger under her chin, forcing her to look at him. "Baby, I'm so sorry I hurt you. My past is where it should have been years ago—in the past. I didn't realize it until recently, but I hadn't started living again until you came along."

Derek dropped his hand and stepped back. He dug through his front pocket and pulled out a white-gold chain, letting it dangle from his hand.

"I've been thinking about a conversation we had a couple months ago."

Macy gazed up at him, aware of the seriousness in his tone. "What conversation?"

"The one where you told me how you wanted to one day get married and have a family."

Anxiety bounced around in Macy's gut. They'd had the conversation so many times, she wasn't sure if he was talking about one particular instance. "Okay," she said on a shaky breath.

"I want that, too. You came into my life at a period when I didn't have time to think about getting serious with someone. As a matter of fact, I had no intention of ever opening my heart to another woman. But here you are. Baby, you have added so much to my life. I'm sorry that I ran scared, but I want us to be together... forever."

"Derek," Macy breathed his name, unsure of what to say. She had waited so long to hear these words from him.

"I want to spend the rest of my life with you. I am so ready to make you my wife. Give me another chance to prove how much I love you and that I'm ready to take our relationship to the next level."

Macy swallowed hard. The love she saw brimming in his eyes matched the love flowing through her body for him. She belonged to him and he belonged to her. And the only way she would ever get that happily-ever-after that she'd longed for was if she took a chance on him. Took a chance on them.

Still holding the chain in his hand, he dug through

his pocket and pulled out a small velvet box. Macy's heart leaped within her chest and tears prickled behind her eyes when Derek got down on one knee. He opened the box to reveal a gorgeous five-carat halo diamond engagement ring surrounded by smaller diamonds along the split-shank band.

"Please say you'll be my wife. Marry me."

She hesitated for a second, but then her head bobbed up and down like a bobblehead. "Yes. Yes, I'll marry you." She wrapped her arms around his neck and he lifted her off the floor as he kissed her sweetly.

"I promise, you won't be sorry," Derek said when he finally set her on her feet. "I'm going to spend the rest of my life making all of your dreams come true."

He pulled the ring from the box.

"What's the chain for?" Macy asked.

"I didn't think you'd be able to wear the ring on your finger right now." He pointed to her cast. "I figured if you said yes, you could wear it around your neck."

Macy laughed, not surprised that he'd thought of everything. After he fastened the chain around her neck, she hugged him again.

"I love you so much," she said. "Thank you for giving me a chance to prove to you that you can trust me with your heart."

Epilogue

One year later

"Hey, sweetheart," Derek said when he walked into Macy's new office where she was nursing their three-month-old baby girl, Amber Price Logan. He leaned down and gave Macy a slow, lazy kiss. He didn't think he would ever get tired of kissing his beautiful wife. "I see she's asleep."

"Well, she was." They both laughed when Amber's eyes popped open and immediately zoned in on Derek. Her toothless grin made his heart clench every time. "You heard Daddy's voice?" Macy kissed the baby's chubby cheek and ran her fingers through her dark, curly hair. Amber looked so much like Jason when he was a baby that in some photos they looked as if they could have been twins.

He lifted his daughter from Macy's arms, giving her a chance to adjust her clothes after breastfeeding. Marrying Macy had been the best thing he had ever done in his life. Not only was she a loving wife, but the way she cared for their children left him in awe. Her energy, compassion and the love that poured out of her never ceased to amaze him. He knew some of it had to do with her growing up in foster care and longing for a family of her own, but she was a natural. It was as if she was born to be a wife and mother.

Amber wiggled in his arms as if knowing that all of his attention wasn't on her.

"How is Daddy's baby girl?" he cooed and pulled a chair up next to Macy's. Amber, named after Macy's patient who had died, as well as Noah, studied him and then grinned. She was such a happy baby.

A few years ago, he had sworn off marriage and having more children. Now he wanted a house full of them. His life had changed for the better over the past year and he owed it all to Noah. Had it not been for his illness, Derek and Macy might not have ever crossed paths.

Derek's gaze landed on his beautiful wife. Sometimes it felt as if his heart would explode from how much he loved her and their children. Staring down at Amber, who'd been born a month early but was in perfect health, Derek didn't think his life could ever be as perfect as it was now.

"Has everyone left?" Macy asked, breaking into

his thoughts. Today they'd had an open house for the Noah Price Medical Complex and had invited family, friends and people from the medical industry, as well as state officials.

"Your sisters are still here." He glanced at his watch. "And actually, the builder we used is supposed to drop something off in about fifteen minutes, so I'm going to meet him out front."

"Daddy! Mommy!" They heard Jason before they saw him.

"Jason, stop running!" Tania called after him.

Derek and Macy shared a look before they started laughing. Their son seemed to run everywhere he went. It was as if he didn't know how to walk.

"Daddy?" he called again.

"In here, son."

"Oh," Jason said when he arrived in the doorway of Macy's office. "Is my sister awake?"

Amber sleepily lifted her head at the sound of Jason's voice. Macy chuckled. Between Derek and her brother's attention, it was a wonder she got any sleep.

"Sorry, I've been trying to keep him busy, but he insisted on checking on his little sister," Tania said from the doorway. "Is it okay if I leave him with you guys?"

"No problem," Macy said to Tania. "We're going back out there in a few minutes anyway."

"You woke Amber up, lil' man." Derek tried placing her head back on his shoulder, but his daughter wasn't having it.

"Daddy, Amber doesn't want to go to sleep." Jason grabbed hold of her little hand and baby-talked with her the way he'd seen Macy and Derek do. Amber giggled as if he was tickling her. "See?"

Derek gave up and sat the baby on his lap, giving her a better view of her brother.

"Can she go to sleep later? I want to take her to see the fish tank." He tried lifting his sister from Derek's lap.

"I don't know where he gets his energy. He is truly *your* child," Derek said, smiling. He leaned over, and covered Macy's lips with his.

"Yes, he is." She pulled Jason in for a hug and as usual, he gladly gave her one back. "He's my big boy." Jason grinned and stuck out his chest.

Derek stood with the baby. "I'm going to go and see if the builder is out front. I'll take the kids with me. Where are you going to be?" he asked Macy.

"I'm going to see if I can find my sisters before they leave. Why don't I meet you in the main hall-way? I'm thinking we should be able to close every-thing up soon."

"Sounds good. I'll see you in a few." He kissed her and they all walked out of the office together.

Moments later, Macy collapsed into the upholstered chair next to Iris. "I'm so tired I think I'm going to sleep for a week."

"I bet you are," her sister said. She rocked one of her one-year-old twins, who was slowly drifting off to sleep. Stephen and Trevon were a handful when they were together, feeding off each other's energy. Yet when they were separate, they were as sweet as could be. "I think it's safe to say that the open house was a success. This place is state-of-the-art and absolutely beautiful. And it seemed as if every elected official was in attendance, along with every doctor and dentist in the state."

"I know, right?" Janna chimed in, glancing at her cell phone before she sat next to Macy in what would be the waiting room. "I'm going to have to think seriously about relocating to Atlanta, considering the number of eligible doctors here."

"Yeah, I saw you downstairs surrounded by all of those fine men. It looked like you were doing a group interview or something." Iris readjusted her son.

Janna laughed and glanced at her cell again. "It's nice to know that I still have it."

Macy and Iris turned to her as if she'd lost her mind.

"Are you kidding me?" Macy asked. "You're a supermodel who most men can only dream of hooking up with. And at twenty-six, with not an ounce of fat on you, I think it's pretty safe to say you're going to have *it* for many years to come."

They all turned when they heard a baby chattering. Nash Dupree strolled toward them, looking every bit the millionaire business mogul that he was. Macy still couldn't believe that the former most eligible bachelor in Atlanta was walking around carrying a diaper bag and a very busy toddler squirming in his arms.

"There's Mommy," Nash said to the twin that he was carrying.

"Hey, there. How're two of my favorite men?" Iris stood, holding a now-sleeping toddler. She and Nash shared a kiss as if they hadn't seen each other in days instead of minutes.

"Oh, get a room already," Janna joked. "I can't believe you guys are still all lovey-dovey even after having these two busy rug rats."

Nash stole another quick peck from his wife before turning his attention to Janna.

"You know, Auntie Janna, if you came to Atlanta more often to babysit, we could spend a little more time playing kissy-face." He kissed Iris again. "As a matter of fact, I think you should agree to babysit tonight," he said between kisses, as if he couldn't get enough of Iris.

Janna rolled her eyes and stood. "You guys are too much, and to make it even worse, I have to watch Macy and Derek do the same thing now." She looked at her cell phone again. She started walking toward the main hallway but stopped and turned. "Oh, and I can't babysit tonight. I have plans. So I guess you're going to have to find another sucker. I mean sitter." They all shared a laugh.

"Wait up, Janna," Macy called after her, stopping her before she got too far ahead. "I take it you're expecting a call? You've glanced at the cell phone about ten times in the past five minutes."

"I am. My agent is working on something big for me and he was supposed to call me hours ago." She continued walking.

"Big like what?"

"An opportunity that I'm not at liberty to discuss just yet."

Macy stopped. Her hand flew to her chest in mock offense. "I'm your sister. You can tell me anything."

"I know, I know, but I need to wait until things are finalized." They started walking again. "And where is my gorgeous niece? I can't believe you let her out of your sight."

"I know. It's never easy."

Macy's heart fluttered at the mention of her baby girl. Even after three months, there were still days she couldn't believe that she had a baby. Lately, she'd been thinking about her biological mother. She didn't know how anyone, especially a mother, could give up their child. Macy could barely stand to be away from Amber and Jason for more than a few hours.

"She and Jason are with Derek. I'm sure we'll run into them before you leave."

Macy smiled, thinking about her husband. All she had wanted was a dose of passion and a family, but she had received so much more from their union. And it was all thanks to Noah Price. He had been instrumental in making her two most important dreams come to fruition: opening a medical complex and having a family. Noah had even left money for her wedding and a trust fund for their firstborn.

Macy and Derek had decided against a long engagement, marrying less than a month after he and Jason came to her office. The memory of that day still brought a smile to her lips. God, she loved that man.

As if thinking him into existence, they saw Derek and the kids at the end of the main hallway near the exit.

"Oh, there they are." Macy turned to Janna, who stopped suddenly. "What's wrong with you?"

"I…I… Do you know who that is Derek is talking to?" Macy didn't miss the shock, or was it fear, she saw in her sister's eyes.

She grabbed Janna's arm at the elbow. "Janna, what's going on? Are you feeling okay?"

"Who is the guy, Macy?" Her words were sharper this time.

"That's Austin Reynolds. He and his family own one of the largest real estate development companies in the country." Janna's hand went to her mouth and Macy moved in closer. "I take it you know him."

"I can't believe it's him," Janna mumbled, her voice shaken.

"Well, why don't you go and say hi?" Macy started pulling her toward the men. Derek and Austin looked up at the same time. There was definite recognition in Austin's gaze, but his eyes narrowed. Macy wasn't sure what the scowl was about, but apparently Janna saw it, too. Instead of moving forward, her sister took a step back.

Austin said something to Derek and then left. Just like that.

"What the heck?" The words tumbled out of Macy's mouth. "What was that all about? I thought you said you knew him."

"I did. It was a long time ago." She ran her hands through her long hair with auburn highlights that fell loosely around her shoulders. "A very long time ago."

"It couldn't have been that long ago. You're only twenty-six." Ten years older than Janna, Macy hadn't known many of Janna's friends while she was growing up.

"We met in high school." Janna reached into the side of her Hermès Birkin handbag. "I'm going to head out. I'll try to stop by the house tomorrow before I leave for New York." They embraced and Janna rushed toward the exit, hugging Derek and the kids before leaving.

"Wow, she looked like she was in a hurry," Derek said when he reached Macy. He cradled Amber in his arm and wrapped his other arm around Macy's waist. Jason bounced around nearby.

"What do you say we get everyone out of here and then go home so we can start working on another baby?"

Macy waggled her eyebrows. "I love it when you talk like that, Daddy. Maybe we can try for two."

"Yeah, Daddy," Jason piped in. "Can I have two brothers like Tania?"

Macy burst out laughing. This kid was too smart for his own good. She'd had no idea he was listening. For a while, they were able to spell everything out, but now that Jason was starting to read, they needed to come up with another way of communicating.

"You know, I like the way you guys think. I'll see what I can do, son." He winked at Jason, who grinned up at him.

Macy's heart swelled. Over a year ago, she'd been about ready to give up on the idea of getting married and having children. Now she was a witness to the fact that dreams really did come true.

* * * * *

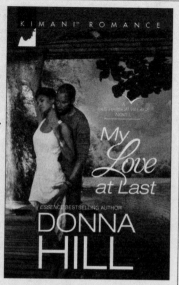

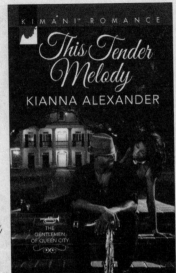

REQUEST YOUR FREE BOOKS!

2 FREE NOVELS PLUS 2 FREE GIFTS!

KIMANI™
ROMANCE

Love's ultimate destination!

The first two
stories in the
Love in the Limelight
series, where four
unstoppable women
find fame, fortune
and ultimately...
true love.

LOVE IN THE LIMELIGHT

New York Times
bestselling author
BRENDA JACKSON
&
A.C. ARTHUR

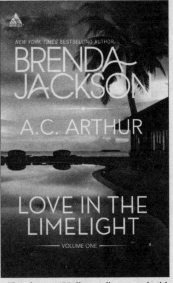

In *Star of His Heart,* Ethan Chambers is Hollywood's most eligible bachelor. But when he meets his costar Rachel Wellesley, he suddenly finds himself thinking twice about staying single.

In *Sing Your Pleasure,* Charlene Quinn has just landed a major contract with L.A.'s hottest record label, working with none other than Akil Hutton. Despite his gruff attitude, she finds herself powerfully attracted to the driven music producer.

Available now wherever books are sold!

H HARLEQUIN®
™ www.Harlequin.com

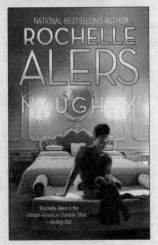

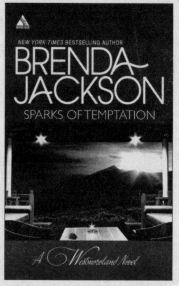

KPBJI700215R